The Unintended

R u sure??

Acknowledgements

I would first like to thank all of my friends who expressed interest and excitement about the news that I was writing a novel. Their excitement was one of many things that kept me going! I deeply want to thank those that were instructive, and constructive, with their critiques and criticisms as they kept me at the project and urged me to do better. I would especially like to thank my wife, Judy, and my eldest son, Mike, for their editing. I would also like to thank Lauren Armstrong for her work and beautiful production of the cover for The Unintended. It is for people like these that I thank God that they are in my life, for I know that I could not have accomplished this alone. I thank them all!

Prologue

As you will notice this story takes place in two distinct centuries with each having a set of characters all its own. The information presented in the late nineteenth century is presented in such a way as to wrap the characters into some of the prevailing political, religious, and social mores of the time. One of the principle references is to Spiritism, which is also referred to as Spiritualism. The Spiritist movement included the practice of séances owing to the belief that members of this movement felt that they could learn things and be comforted by the past experiences of deceased relatives and friends and then relate them to the hardships that they encountered in their own lives. As in any time in history there were those that would capitalize on the gullible and unsuspecting. The Spiritist Movement moved away from the very distinct Victorian sentiments of the day and did so in some dramatic ways. One of those ways was the sharing of spouses sexually. Not surprisingly, since there was a lack of information as to when a woman's fertile time of the month was and a lack of birth control methods, many unwanted pregnancies needed to be dealt with. In fact, around the year 1860, it is estimated that six- hundred thousand Spiritist women had terminated their pregnancies.

It was not only Spiritist women that were having abortions. Many women who were now at home raising the family while their husbands were *out in the world* at work were also inclined to have them. Again, due to an absence of adequate birth control and ignorance of the fertile time in their menstrual cycles, they often found themselves pregnant with the prospects of another mouth to feed and another child to take care of often with inadequate finances of the wage–earner, their husbands. In order for many of these women to escape increasing hardship upon themselves they often resorted to abortion and even infanticide. The practice had become so common that it is estimated that one in five to one in six pregnancies were aborted between the years 1850 and 1860, with at times deadly results for the mother as well. There were some liberated practitioners, not always doctors, who found a living performing these procedures. Some had more stellar outcomes than others. One of those practitioners who is referenced in the book, but by a different name, is Madame Restell, who owned a large estate on Fifth Avenue in New York City.

By the 1870s all states had criminalized abortions and the American Medical Association denounced the procedure. Prior to that, the laws varied from state to state. But in New York City, which was the setting for the characters in the nineteenth century, the laws were quite stiff for the perpetrators of abortion so it was best not to be caught with evidence. And despite laws against abortion, the smaller papers of the day, referred to as *The Penny Press,* continued to run ads for the termination of pregnancies but did so delicately by using such phrases as *restoring monthly regularity.*

At the same time, there was a rise in both men and women who spoke out politically about the lack of rights for women. Not only was there a start in the debate, often heated, about the right to vote but also about wives ability to own things in their own name. Up until this time any wages that a wife earned were the property of her husband and, as the stories go, some of the husbands felt comfortable and justified relying on their wives to earn the household money. They would then use the money in whatever manner they wished and often not for the household. Those non–household uses often include vices. In that era men were also allowed to legally beat their wives for reasons of their own. If he were to use a stick to do so he could use one no larger than the width of his thumb. Interestingly, that is where the *Rule Of Thumb* originated.

There were times when social issues were discussed amongst members at Spiritist meetings. These discussions often preceded the mediums contact with the spirit world. Several references are made to this type of activity in the book.

Overall, much was changing in this period in history and the time was ripe for an upheaval in social mores and customs. This could be partially explained by a shift from rural communities to increasingly centralized urban industrial factory work. In the one instance large families were needed to help support the family and children were only taught the necessities. When work moved away from the farms, and the father worked away from the home, families that could afford to send their sons to school would do so, and the girls would be schooled at home by their mothers. The girls from wealthier families would receive formal schooling also. This separation of the man from his home in order to work engendered what was called the *Two Spheres,* where the man was out in the world with work, business and potential corruption and the woman was at home with the duty to keep herself, the home and her children morally pure. Women were expected to maintain moral superiority, maintain fidelity and to keep her man in the sphere of duty, charity, virtue, religion and peace. This wasn't always the case as some women needed to also enter the industrialized workforce. However, for the most part, the two sphere concept was the ideal. This idealized way of looking at the world lent itself to criticism from individuals that were more progressive.

Some of the major players in the move for women's rights included Elizabeth Cody Stanton, Susan B. Anthony, Sarah Grimke, Phoebe Palmer, and the Bronte sisters. Elizabeth Stanton was known not only for women's rights but also for advocating for the abolition of slavery. Her *Declaration of Sentiments* was felt to be sentinel in initiating the first women's rights movement in the United States. Susan B. Anthony co-established *The Revolution*–a women's rights journal–and was known to speak on women's rights at the rate of one hundred speeches per year. Sarah Grimke spoke out against slavery. Ironically, her father was a slave-owner. She was often found teaching her father's slaves to read and was often reprimanded for it. The book Jane Eyre, written by Charlotte Bronte, represented independence of women at a time when it was not accepted. As an example, the main character, Jane, after she marries, refused to rely on her husband for her welfare and even refused his lavish gifts. She preferred to earn her own keep and continue her work as a governess.

The reference to the play "Our American Cousin" is included for a couple of reasons. It was a popular play of the time, and for historical purposes, was the play that President Abraham Lincoln attended when he was assassinated.

In the part of the story set in the present time the varied views on abortion currently held in the United States are reflected to some degree in the family of the book's main character – Ginny Chandler. Also presented is a possible consequence of her decision to proceed with the procedure and the effects on her as well as other family members. There is debate as to whether an intentional termination of pregnancy will cause psychological effects. One may cite various medical papers that state with some clarity the effects shown in Ginny, as well as other effects which include depression and increased suicide risk and ideation.

In the end, the reader is left to make his or her own conclusions about what is revealed in the latter stages of the book and to debate the relevance of what seems to be two independent stories, but are they, and one seemingly truncated–or is it?

Chapter One

The gas lights on the street were just starting to be lit on a cold mid–November day in New York City. The year was 1860 and Samuel and Elsa Ulrich were on their way to a new adventure, or should I say experience, for which they were both apprehensive and nervously excited.

"The weather is a bit colder than I remember for this time of year, don't you think, Sam?"

"Perhaps, dear, but it could just be the stiff wind that bites through right down to the bone. We probably should have taken the carriage rather than walk, but too late now. I agree with you though. I am out and about every day of the week and it does seem that the cold weather has arrived early this year. I hope Dr. Cribbs has stoked a fine fire this evening."

"That would be exceedingly nice. I hope he has also."

"I did tell you that he expects about three other couples besides us tonight, did I not?"

"Yes you did, and I believe that this is about the third time that you have. I think that you may be just a bit more excited about this than I am!"

"Perhaps, I am rather intrigued by this spiritualistic movement that is growing not only here but across the Atlantic!"

The Ulrich's hope for warmth was answered because there was a large fireplace at the Cribbs' residence with a well–stoked fire already burning when they arrived.

Dr. Cribbs directed Bessie, a maid–servant, to attend to his guests coats. "It is so nice to meet you Mrs. Ulrich. I have heard a bit about you from your husband. I would like so much to hear more about you and your family here in New York. Come on in and please meet John and Sarah Hughs and Thomas and Mary Kent. The last couple, August and Beverly Frederick should be arriving soon."

Soon was almost immediately, for no sooner had Dr. Cribbs announced their names than the Fredericks arrived. Mrs. Frederick was petite, very pretty and deferring. She was easily lost under the bold countenance of her husband. Mr. Frederick immediately went about introducing himself and his wife to the other guests without waiting for Dr. Cribbs to do the formal introductions. When he got to the Ulriches he seemed to take a bit more time as he was quite transfixed by Elsa. Elsa embarrassingly removed her eyes from August's gaze and she quickly looked to see if Samuel had been watching. Samuel had been saying hello to Mrs. Frederick and did not witness August's seeming interest in his wife.

"It is time to sit down and enjoy a meal and conversation before we get to the main portion of the evening. Bessie, please escort our guests to the dining room and show them to their seats," announced Dr. Cribbs.

The meal was not uncommon but was immensely flavorful. "Who is the wonderful and masterful cook?" exclaimed Mr. Frederick. "Let me kiss the hand of this genius for the soup was exquisite, the roasted pork and potatoes divine, the squash and dinner rolls magnificent, the citrus ice sublime and the dessert from out of this dimension."

"You're just looking to be invited back for dinner" Mr. Kent retorted.

Everyone around the table joined in laughter. As they were enjoying coffee Dr. Cribbs asked Elsa about her family. She explained that she was an only child and that her father had been in finance.

"What do you mean by had been in finance?" asked the doctor. "Is he involved in another occupation currently?"

"Both of my parents passed due to influenza about twelve years ago."

"I am so sorry to hear that. But yes, the epidemic! How could I forget that? So many people did not survive that pestilence! That must have been so devastating to you! You must have been quite young at the time. Who continued to raise you?"

"My uncle and aunt took me in, and since I was old enough to go to a boarding school, that is where they sent me. I studied to become a teacher which I am today. I teach at Philos Seminary which is not far from here. But I believe you knew that I am a teacher?"

"Yes I did, but I did not know that you taught locally and for a Christian school. Did you know your aunt and uncle well when all this happened?"

"No, I had only met them once. They did not have any children and seemed content without any from what I knew from my parents."

"Did they receive you well into their household?"

"Oh, they were kind but it was not long before I was off to the boarding school in Philadelphia. I forgot to mention, they lived in Philadelphia."

"I suspect that you miss your parents."

"I miss them dearly and I think about them almost daily in my quiet moments. I think about how my life would be if they did not become ill, though I also wonder if I would have met my dear husband Samuel if their unfortunate fate to the influenza did not happen. I feel almost guilty for feeling that way but . . ." Elsa drifted briefly into remembrances of her mother and father. "Did you know Dr. Cribbs that Samuel had his pharmaceutical training in Philadelphia?"

While Dr. Cribbs was engaged in conversation with Elsa the remainder of the party was getting well acquainted with each other. The only person not doing much talking was Mrs. Kent. It wasn't that she wasn't attentive. In fact it seemed as though she was almost tuned into everything.

There was a knock at the front door. Bessie went to answer and a young woman of about 25 years of age and alone was escorted in. Dr. Cribbs introduced Sally Cooke to his guests and informed them that she was to be their contact to the spirit world tonight. Bessie showed Miss Cooke to a room where she could prepare.

"Let us raise a glass to good friendships, prosperity and success with our endeavors this evening," the doctor toasted before he led his guests into the parlor for the rest of the evening's activities.

The Cribbs' parlor was bigger than the dining room but not immense. There was another fireplace which merged into the same chimney as the fireplace in the adjacent room. As in the first room there was already a fire burning. There were also flowers of several types in vases placed on various small tables throughout the room. On the walls were some paintings with large ships that one would guess carried immigrants over to the Americas. In addition to the flowers on the tables were daguerreotypes of what possibly could be friends or relatives of the doctor and his wife. Some of the people were older and some younger but most seemed to be similar in apparent age as the doctor and his wife. In the middle of the room was an approximately six foot round table with nothing on it at all.

Mr. Frederick inquired of Dr. Cribbs who the people in the pictures were. The doctor indicated that they were some good and close friends from his medical training as well as relatives, some now deceased.

"I am sure many of them are renowned, just as yourself" said Mr. Frederick.

"Thank you for your compliment and yes, many of them are. The pictures are here so that I can be reminded of them frequently. As time goes by our memories can often fade of those acquaintances that we may never see again and of those that are passed into the realm beyond. They are all very significant in my life due to the knowledge and good advice that they have imparted to me."

The Ulriches were starting to feel the same excited nervousness again that they had earlier. The other guests had been to meetings like this before, and even though they also were somewhat nervous about what they were about to experience, they were certainly more comfortable than the Ulriches.

"Sam, do you really think that this is okay to do? I am getting really nervous!"

"It will be alright. I will be right beside you." With a wry smile he also said, "My loving arms are ready to encircle you if you come into harm's way."

"Please do not kid with me," Elsa answered quickly and with a bit of annoyance.

Both Doctor Cribbs and Mr. Frederick noticed what now looked to be true anxiety in Elsa's eyes. Dr. Cribbs spoke up quickly to allay any fear, saying, "You need to know that if we make contact tonight with our loved ones beyond, they will mean us no harm. Not always are we successful in our attempts to reach who we wish, but when reached, there should be nothing revealed to us that should terrify us."

Before settling down around the table Elsa made the sign of the cross and said a prayer for protection. She also made sure that she stayed very close to her husband. Even though she felt a bit comforted by the doctor's words she was still very apprehensive.

By the time Sally Cooke appeared the gas lights in the room had been extinguished and only a few candles were left to give sufficient light so as to be able to distinguish who was in the room. Miss Cooke wore a white flowing gossamer gown and appeared ephemeral with the soft glow of a nearby candle highlighting her pale and heavenly smooth skin. A loose ringlet of flowers circled the crown of her head allowing long ringlets of hair to flow over her face and shoulders.

Speaking slowly and clearly, Sally said to them "I want to let all of you know that there is nothing to be afraid of. I can already feel that all of you have had persons who have been very special in your lives who have passed on. They may have passed away from the earth but they are not fully gone. They want to reach out to you and help you in any way they can and they may have very personal information to tell you. I have been given the gift to help us connect with those in the spirit realm and this is what I need all of you to do. I ask that you put yourselves at ease and concentrate on the person that you want to connect with while remembering them as they were when they were alive. There may be many reasons for wanting to reach them. It may be that you need to know that they are still there. Or it could be that you want to say a good bye from this earthly life if you did not have that chance when they were still here. You may be looking for an answer to a question for which you feel they may have the answer. Think about what you may want to say because you may only get a brief time to connect. It mostly depends on the level of your connectedness and concentration. Their bodies may be long buried but their spirits are still alive. If you have successfully connected with them you will notice a change in me over which I have no control. I cannot truly tell you exactly how this will happen or exactly in what form that I will be used. But, again, do not be afraid of this transformation for it is how the spirits will communicate with you. You may also see or hear things happening in this room that are caused by the movement of their spirit forces."

Sarah Hughs asked, "If I would like to reach more than one spirit is that possible?"

John, her husband, whispered to Thomas, "Never content with one, always expecting an audience!"

There was slight laughter from Thomas before Sally, who was already feeling a change in her consciousness, responded, "It is best to try to only communicate with one loved one at a time and put your full effort into concentrating on them. Please concentrate on that specific loved one that you wish to encounter tonight." With that Sally's face became still and her gaze appeared to look into oblivion. There was a sudden flickering of the candles and a crackling of the logs in the fireplace. Elsa noticed that the only window in the room was opened at the bottom but had not been that way when they sat down. She was the only one to notice the open window. She was finding it hard to concentrate due to not knowing what could happen and now she was really beside herself. She was horrified! She grabbed tightly to her husband, startling him. He, a chill running up and down his spine thinking that he was contacted by the spirit of the person he was concentrating on, quickly turned wide eyed and in panic in the direction of the squeeze. He quickly found that he was staring right into Elsa's panicked eyes and he threw his arms around her in an attempt to keep her safe.

Sally swiftly drew everyone's attention when she said, "A sister spirit has entered the room. She says that she is seeking Mary."

Mary Kent, remarked as if surprised, "Oh Missy! I can't believe it! Dear sister why did you leave? I so miss you."

"You do not know what I suffered in life due to my husband, who I do wish is in hell! I should be also. He would only let me leave the house on Sundays to go to worship services. No enjoyment! Do this, do that! What a life! When I did not do something exactly as he wanted, he beat me. That is why I did not always see you on Sundays. I had to heal from my wounds. But I showed him. I cooked him his favorite meal but added a little extra ingredient. Oh, and he never recovered. So sad. Boo hoo. I was so distraught about what I had done, even though I knew he deserved it, that I had to hang myself! How I am not in hell I have no clue."

"No, no, you cannot be telling me the truth!" protested Mary.

"Oh no! Remember that dead men tell no lies, dear sister. Do not be disturbed for I am free and in no pain. Hallelujah."

"Who is this that is joining us now, for I feel another presence?" asked Sally. "James, you say that you are looking for James?"

With delight and excitement Dr. Cribbs exclaimed, while at the same time giving his old friend the business, "Curtis! Hey good friend. I had heard that you got the typhus. You couldn't take care of yourself, you quack?"

"Is that how you are going to treat an old medical school chap, Jimmy boy? You've got the nerve. Who is it that got you through anatomy class?" Curtis cuttingly asked. "Yes, me! You would never be where you are now if it were not for me!"

"Are you serious? You wouldn't know a liver from a spleen," retorted James Cribbs.

"This is how you talk to someone that was a friend of yours, James?" asked Samuel.

"Don't worry with how we talk to each other. We know it is all in good fun. I know how concerned you and Elsa were with reaching out to the spirit world but now you see it can be quite fun and not scary. Remember, I told you that there was nothing to worry about."

"James, did you forget about me? You know that I can't stay here all night. If you continue drifting off talking to your live people I will have to wander off."

"Can't you join me in my conversation with the others?" James asked Curtis.

"Well, mm, I guess. I have never done that before."

"First time for everything Curtis!"

"Okay, so let me tell you about the first day I met James. It was in anatomy class. Yes, the class that James would not have passed if it were not for me. We met at our cadaver and the first thing we did after introducing ourselves to each other was to introduce ourselves to our body. We named her G l o r i a ..."

As Curtis was speaking his words came out slower and slower and quieter and quieter and at the same time Sally Cooke seemed to be starting to come out of her trance–like state. Suddenly Curtis was gone and the window shut with a slam.

It took a bit of time for Sally to fully recover but when she did she said, "Tell me what happened".

Sarah said, "Don't you know what happened? You had two spirits talking right out of your mouth! One was Mary's sister and the other a doctor friend of James named Curtis."

Jessica Cribbs continued by saying, "Mary's sister, Missy . . . . Oh, you do not mind, Mary, that I let Miss Cooke know what was said, do you?"

"Since everyone else here heard what my sister said I suppose it does not matter, but I am rather upset by what she informed me of. I never would have thought my sister would do such a thing. But since she said it right out in front of everyone in this room I guess she did not care that everyone heard it!"

Jessica continued, "Mary's sister, Missy, said that she was beaten by her husband frequently, and when she had had enough she put something in his food and he died. She was in such a state afterward that she hanged herself."

Mary suggested a reason for her deceased sister's action, saying, "Her husband must have been a real fiend at home for Missy to do what she did for he never seemed that way when we were all together. And for her to be spared the pangs of hell with what she did, he must have been a real monster to her."

Sarah then went on to say, "And a friend of Dr. Cribbs even got as bold as to address conversation to the rest of the group at the urging of Dr. Cribbs. He was quite funny and good natured."

"He sounded like quite the comedian", added August Frederick.

Dr. Cribbs then turned to Samuel and Elsa and asked 'What did you think of your first foray into the spirit world with a medium?"

Samuel spoke first and said, "Besides initially being apprehensive, and then scared to the dickens by what I thought was a spirit grabbing me . . ."

"A spirit actually grabbed you?" asked Sally. "That would be a first for me. That is exciting!"

"It turned out to be me," pronounced Elsa giddily. "I literally felt like I jumped right out of my skin when I saw the window open and the candles flicker and heard the fireplace crackle. I grabbed on tightly to Samuel and he reacted just as he said he would and held on to me."

Sarah said, "I wish that John did that for me at my first séance because I was really scared too. That was so sweet. I wish I would have seen all that! I was concentrating so much on the spirit that I wanted to meet that I did not even hear or see anything until the first spirit, Mary's sister's spirit, that is, started talking."

***

Thomas and Mary Kent were the last to leave the Cribbs' residence that night. On their carriage ride home as they cuddled together for warmth, Mary said to her husband, "Tom, I am so glad that you were finally able to slip out and unlock that window before we all sat down for the séance."

"Don't you mean medium–enhanced meeting of the spirit world?" Thomas said as he laughed.

Mary answered Thomas, grinning, "Yes, indeed! I tell you, we sure struck a gem when we found Sally. She is good!"

"Yes, her costuming and her eerie trance–like state really get you into the mood immediately when you see her, and then that slow mesmerizing voice, gadzooks! Yes indeed, a winner."

Chapter Two

Ginny Chandler came home from high school and was heading straight to her bedroom. Her mother heard her come in and said from the kitchen, "Ginny, is that you? I need you to cook dinner for your father and brothers tonight because I am catching an extra shift at Luciana's."

"Oh, okay mom, I can do that."

"Come in the kitchen and talk to me."

Ginny walked into the kitchen as her mom was pulling all the ingredients that Ginny would need. She asked her mom, "When are you going to eat?"

"Don't worry about me. I'll throw something down at the restaurant when I get a chance. How was your day?"

"It was all right. It was announced that tryouts for the sophomore cheerleading squad will be this Friday."

"Are you going to try out?"

"Yeah, I think so. Is that all right? I got a C on my English paper that I got back today and I wasn't sure if you would be okay with me trying out."

Mrs. Chandler answered while she was putting on her makeup, "I know that you try hard to get good grades. Maybe a diversion would be good for you. It may just get you better at managing your time. I don't have a problem with it?"

"What about Dad?"

"I will talk to him about it, so don't say anything to him. Well, I better get going. I probably won't see you until tomorrow since I will be home very late. Get your beauty sleep. Remember that a good night's rest does wonders for your health, and your memory, too! See you."

Ginny, short for Virginia, was what she was called from the earliest she could remember. Even when her parents needed to be stern with her she was called Ginny and not the usual Virginia as would be common for most parents to do. They did add the usual middle name and for Ginny that would be Anne. So they might say, "Ginny Anne, if you . . . ." But, she was a good girl, somewhat shy, very pretty, with soft and appealing facial features. Her parents rarely had reason to be upset with her. Her only problem was that she had a tough time doing well in school. She was not dumb, but she just didn't grasp concepts as quickly as others. She learned more by experience than by books, or should I say, the written word. Her father was mindful of and stressed a good education. He believed doing well in school was the means to prosperity.

Her father, Alex Chandler, did not apply himself well to his studies either when he was in school but was still able to do above average work and get accepted to a good university based on his excellent test scores. When his father died from a truck driving accident when he was about to start university, being the oldest of seven children, he put off his education to help his mother earn for the family. Being his father was a truck driver, he had gained a lot of his knowledge of motor vehicle repair by helping his dad repair his truck when needed. That was more frequent than either one of them desired, but since the family always seemed to be living on a shoestring his father could not afford to purchase a new truck. Alex had also done a lot of reading in auto repair journals and did work on late model cars of his own. He had even worked part–time at a friend's father's auto shop while in high school and was able to be hired on full–time after his father's unfortunate demise. He worked hard for his family but always felt that life could have been much different if he were to have gone further than high school with his education. He believed that it would have been so much easier to provide what his own family needed if his earning power were greater. Being as it was his wife Rosaria had to contribute to the family's financial earnings and she did so without complaining because she agreed with Alex that her children should be given a full opportunity to achieve the potential they each had with the abilities that they were created with.

As a parent, Rosaria – Rose as she preferred – was much more comforting and consoling than Alex. Whereas Rose would talk through a disappointment–whether scholastic or personal – with her children, Alex would be firm and opinionated with his remarks, especially involving poor grades or personal choices. His children quickly learned that it was often better to ask mom's opinion rather than his. Certainly Ginny did. Brian, Ginny's older brother by two years, seemed to never raise the ire of his father. He was the ultimate student in grade school and in high school. He was even ranked academically in the top two percent of his class. Therefore, Brian never really had to concern himself about what his father might say because his classwork was stellar. Martin, the youngest of the three children, was special in his own way. He was handsome, had an athletic build, even as a young child, and had a way of dealing with people so as to not have to work very hard to get what he needed. Marty, as he preferred to be called, was six years younger than Brian and four years younger than Ginny. How the children turned out so differently was anyone's guess. Many of Rose's friends had different theories ranging from too few vitamins with one child to too little nursing with another. She did have to wonder if the fish oil supplements had anything to do with Brian's intelligence. If it did, it paid off big time. Rose was not about to play the game of comparing

14

her children, though. Hers was to love each one of them for who they were because she knew that she could not change anything of the past.

"Dad, is that you?"

"Yes, Ginny, where is your mother?"

"She had to work at the restaurant tonight. She picked up an extra shift. How was your day today?"

"Everything went okay. It has just been a little busy with everyone expecting the work on their cars to be done yesterday! What are we doing for dinner tonight?"

"Oh, Mom left me the recipe and the ingredients for chili. I've made it before so you don't have to worry. The last time I made it I did not kill anyone. I don't even think I made anyone sick!"

"Well that is good to hear. Where are the boys?"

"I think I heard Brian say this morning that he had a chess meet today and wouldn't know what time he would be home. I guess it would depend if he were winning or not and you know Brian."

"How about Marty?" Ginny's dad answered knowing what she had meant concerning Brian. He probably had been winning.

"I'm not sure, but it could be that soccer practice may have already started."

"If it has I'm sure he will have a large appetite when he gets home. You better make more than the usual amount of that chili tonight! By the way, how was your day today? Any results on that English paper yet?"

"No, not yet." She remembered that her mother had said not to bring up anything to her dad about her grade or about trying out for the cheerleading squad.

"Well, I hope that your grades this year will turn out much better than last year."

Under her breath, Ginny said "I can only hope so, too."

"I'm going to go watch the news. Let me know when dinner is ready."

"Sure thing, Dad." Ginny knew that her dad liked a lot of spice and so made sure that she added a bit extra of the chili powder. She had cooked many times with her mother and found she was good at it and enjoyed it. In fact she would say she was very good at it.

***

It was late afternoon and Marty was at a friend's house playing the newest video game, 'Make My Day-8'. "Hey, this is so much more fun than the last version. There are a lot more encounters for battle and it's more realistic", remarked Scott, Marty's best friend.

"Yeah, that rooftop battle was awesome with those bodies falling over the edge and hitting the ground! Super cool", remarked Marty. "At that soccer meeting today, did the coach say that we had to have the fifty dollars in by Friday?" Marty then asked Scott.

"Yes, along with the permission slip," added Scott.

"Well, I better get going. My parents don't like it when I am late for dinner. Plus I need to act responsible so my mom and dad will cough up the cash for soccer."

"Economic sanctions on Iran have been eased in an attempt to further promote ongoing nuclear agreements with the Iranian Government," a news correspondent stated on the evening International News.

"Reagan would never have allowed this", shouted Alex, sitting in his lazy chair. "First it's meth labs in nursing homes and now this news from the U. N.! Have we lost our minds?" Just then Marty walked through the door. "That was a short soccer practice," Alex chimed.

"Oh, it wasn't practice yet. We had a meeting and coach told us what is expected of us. He told us to always be on time for practice and to be respectful to the refs. He also said that he knows that parents can't always make the games but said that he expects us at all games unless there is a very good excuse, like, like having to save the world from annihilation."

"And what recent video games have you been playing?" asked Ginny, hearing the conversation from the kitchen while she was preparing dinner.

"Scott and me . . ."

"That is Scott and I," corrected Marty's dad.

"Okay, Scott and I just got done playing 'Make My Day-8'."

"When were you at Scott's, son?"

"We had time after the meeting to stop at his house before I came home. He just got the game and we haaad to play it! Anyway, coach said that it will be fifty dollars for the uniforms and equipment this year. Oh, and you have to sign a permission slip."

"I have to sign a permission slip and give you fifty dollars, huh? I don't believe in *have tos*. What are you going to do for me if I do that for you? How about you improve at least one of your B's to an A this year and if not, I bench you? How 'bout that?"

"Are you serious, dad?"

"I couldn't be more serious. When do you need the cash and the permission slip?"

"This Friday."

"Remind me on Thursday night. Let me see that permission slip now so that I can sign it right away. Don't you dare lose it because I don't want to hear about having to sign another."

"I'll make a copy of it and will hang it on the fridge."

"Good idea, smarty," Alex said, intentionally combining smart with his son's name thinking he was quite clever. Neither Marty or Ginny caught it.

"It's time for dinner, dad", Ginny announced. "Marty, would you mind getting some tablespoons and napkins."

"Sure sis, anything else you need?"

"Yes, bring some extra chili powder so that you and dad can add it if you need it. I think it tastes good right now but you both may want some extra."

"Is it the way your mother makes it?" asked her father.

"Yes it is. She left all the ingredients out for me and I double checked to make sure that I had everything before I started."

"Very good because your mother makes the BEST chili east of the Rio Grande."

"How about west of the Rio Grande, dad?" Marty questioned.

"There is some pretty darn good chili in those parts, but I can tell you your mother's recipe would give them a good run for their money."

"And how do you know that, dad? How many places west of the Rio Grande have you had chili?"

"Maybe one, but my father used to say that about my mother's chili and your mom's is just as good, if not better, than hers was. He used to drive his rig to the southwest every few weeks and he ate at a heck of a lot of truck stops." Alex stopped talking to taste a spoonful. "Oooeee! That's some very good and spicy chili! No need for that extra chili powder. Your mother sure did teach you well!"

***

Brian did not get home until eight o'clock that night. He had gotten to the final in the chess meet, only to lose to the reigning champ for the past three years. "You look irritated", Alex said to his oldest son.

"I am. I lost the final chess match to Charlie Michaels. But, I am determined to win the next time we play. Is there any dinner?"

"Yes, your sister made chili tonight."

"Sis? Where is mom tonight?"

Alex answered his son saying, "Yes, your sister made dinner," and then answered Brian's second question with, "Your mother is working an extra shift at Luciana's tonight."

"Well, I am going to pack down some of that chili and then I have to get to my homework. I have a decent amount tonight."

***

Meanwhile, Ginny was trying to tackle biology and photosynthesis. "Let's see, light and carbon dioxide and water give you . . . I know . . . a headache! Heck, I can't remember. How am I going to pass this test? If I could only just put these ingredients in a pan, put them in the oven and then see it make what it is supposed to make, maybe I would get it. I wish I were as smart as Brian."

Brian was just walking out of his bedroom to go to the bathroom when he heard his sister. He said to her, "Can I talk to you sis?"

"Sure Brian, maybe you can get me out of my misery."

"Okay, I'll be right there."

"I sure hope that you washed your hands!" Ginny said after hearing a flush from the bathroom just before Brian walked into her room.

"Well, sure I did. I am not gross. You want help or not?"

"Dad's going to kill me if I don't get a good grade on this biology test tomorrow. I only got a C on my English paper. I just don't understand how it is so easy for you and I can't seem to 'get it' no matter how hard I try."

"Calm down and I will try to help you."

"How can I calm down? Dad never lets up on me. After dinner tonight he told me to go right to my room and study until I could study no longer because he did not want to see anymore D's or F's this year."

"Can you blame him?"

"Yes, because I just can't do this stuff," Ginny said dejectedly.

"What is it that you're trying to study?"

"That stupid photosynthesizer or something."

"Okay, let's first get the word correct. That is pho–to–syn–the–sis. You were almost right. Maybe you need to approach this like you were looking at a recipe."

"I tried that, but I can't remember what I am supposed to get out of the ingredients!"

"Let's try adding a little math to try to help you. Okay, let's say we take the energy of the sunlight and put in 6 molecules of carbon dioxide, that is 6 CO_2 and then add 6 molecules of water, which is 6 H_2O . . ."

***

A few days later Brian asks Ginny what she got on her biology exam and she told him, "I just don't get it. I thought I had it down perfectly but instead of 6 carbon dioxides and 6 waters there were 12 of each and it just didn't work!"

"So, what did you get on the exam?"

"I got another C. The teacher told me that I had the concept right but my math was wrong. Dad's going to yell at me again!"

"You said it was only if you got D's or F's."

"You know that he won't be satisfied with this, not with you and Marty always getting A's and B's!"

"But don't you think that you made some progress? I mean you did get the concept right. Your teacher said so."

"Brian, all I did was memorize what you told me. I don't think my brain can handle all the things I need to memorize to get good grades!"

"Sis, I will continue to help you as much as I can," but Brian was also thinking to himself, *what is she going to do when I am gone at College next year?*

"Thanks, Brian, I love you for doing this for me."

Chapter Three

"Did Ginny mention to you that she wanted to try out for the cheerleading squad this year?" Rose asked Alex as he was reading his newest edition of *Car and Mechanic Magazine*. He didn't fully hear what she had said since he was concentrating on the newest improvements that had been developed in fuel injection systems but he did hear something about cheerleading.

"What did you say about cheerleading?"

This was the first time that Rose had had a free moment to talk to her husband alone about Ginny wanting to try out for cheerleading since she and Ginny had discussed it. By that time, Ginny had already tried out. Rose thought that if he was concentrating so hard on reading that perhaps she could just quickly state that Ginny had tried out and maybe he wouldn't react to it. She thought better of that and felt it best that she explain to Alex how she felt and about what she thought may help Ginny. "I said," and then stopped short and said, "Now please pay attention honey. This is important."

Alex put down the magazine now that he knew Rose really wanted his attention. He had all of his free Saturday to read it anyway. "Okay, what's the problem?"

"It really is not a problem. What I said was Ginny wanted to try out for the cheerleading squad this year and I wondered if she had told you about it?"

"No, she didn't, and if she did I would have told her NO. How can she go off and add another activity if she is having a hard enough time getting decent grades. You know that she won't be able to get into a good college after high school if she doesn't do better! It is important that she get an excellent education and one that goes further than high school!"

"I know that's important to you."

"You know damn well it is!"

"Please simmer down, I'd rather the kids not hear this and I would prefer that we discuss this without so much emotion."

Alex collected himself, lowered his voice, and said, "But you know how important it is for me that the kids go further than high school. I didn't work out for me and I didn't go to college like I had wanted and now we both have to work long hours. You, two jobs! Just to be able to give our kids what they need. I want them to have opportunities and to have things better than us!"

"I understand where you are coming from, but I know that Ginny tries to do well and she gets quite upset when she doesn't. She gets upset because she doesn't feel she can get good grades and she knows that you will get mad at her if she doesn't. Why don't you just let up on her?"

"Let up on her?" his voice rising in volume again.

Ginny was awake and heard the louder parts, the non – whispered ones. And now the boys were awakened by the increased volume of conversation.

"Can't she see that I have pushed all of them to get good grades because it's for their own good?"

Rose, trying to get her husband to lower his voice again, said in almost a whisper, "She sees it as you being mad and disappointed with her when she tries and still fails. Anyway,

I think it would be good for her to go out for cheerleading. I think it may give her some confidence and give her a chance to make some new friends. Who knows, maybe something different will help her? Isn't it worth a try?"

Chapter Four

Alex had finally given in to his wife's arguments concerning Ginny's trying out for the cheerleading squad. It was Sunday now and she was supposed to find out on Monday whether she had made it. She thought she'd done a good job at the try out but knew that it wasn't only doing well that counted. She had friends in the past that were very good but didn't make it, so she knew that talent wasn't all that mattered. She prayed that her natural physical ability would get her through.

Rose came to Ginny's room to talk, knowing it would be safe there, since Alex had gone out to the garage to work. "I spoke to your father about the cheerleading."

"I know. I could hear you both talking about it yesterday, or should I say yelling about it! At least Dad was." Ginny said dejectedly. "I knew deep down that there was no chance!"

"Can you let me finish?" Rose said after Ginny started to settle down. "I was trying to tell you that he is going to allow it." "

Are you serious, mom? I can't believe it! What did he say about my C in English?"

"M-m-m-m, I forgot to mention that. That will just have to be between us. I won't tell if you won't tell, okay?"

"I'm so excited! Does he know that I already tried out?"

"Why does he need to know that?" her mom asked. "I hope that you made the team but we don't really know for sure if

26

you did. Why rile him up for something he doesn't need to know?"

Ginny thought for a second and then said, "And no strings attached, like when he told Marty that if he does not increase a grade from a B to an A that that he was going to bench him?"

"When did this happen? Oh-h--h, never mind that now. No, he didn't put down any rules on this."

"Mom . . ., thank you. You're the best!"

Chapter Five

"We would be more than happy hosting the next meeting at our home, Thomas," said Dr. Cribbs.

"That is most delightful," answered Thomas. "We had such a wonderful time at your home on the previous occasion."

"Thank you, good man. I was thinking after our last encounter that it would be nice to allow more time before having our medium . . . oh, you will arrange for Ms. Cooke again, won't you? She was excellent! Anyway, getting back to what I was about to say. The missus and I would enjoy taking more time before Ms. Cooke gets started to engage in conversation with the rest of our new friends. We'd loved to find out more about them, and I am sure, they about us. Would you agree, Thomas?"

"I believe that that would be a genuinely good idea. Why don't you let the Ulriches know about our next meeting and I will let the Hughses and Frederickses know. I suspect that you and Sam Ulrich often speak, on a professional level at least, he being a pharmacist and you a doctor in town? When shall I say this next meeting will be, Doctor?"

"Let us say a half a fortnight from tomorrow, Saturday. I will tell my wife to make the adequate preparations."

"Good, and I will make arrangements with Miss Cooke," answered Thomas.

Sally Cooke was now doing quite well for herself channeling spirits. She was becoming well known and she was not always easy to book for a séance.

Later that same day, Thomas Kent visited Miss Cooke's apartment and asked, "Sally, the same group that you mediated for a fortnight ago would like you to help us again eight days from now. Can you join us?"

Thinking that she could make a little bit more money than usual she said, "My schedule is getting quite full and I am not sure that I can get free."

Thomas, wanting to seize the opportunity to solidify a solid business relationship with Miss Cooke said, "Will you do it if I pay you a bit more handsomely?"

"It depends on how handsome it is!"

"I'll give you an additional four bits", he answered quickly.

She thought for a moment and then said "Why sure, it is nice to feel appreciated", and to herself, *and also get paid for it.*

"Same time then, around 7:30 pm, as long as that fits your schedule?" Thomas asked with a little bit of humorous sarcasm just to seem playful.

"Oh, yes, but of course, Mr. Kent."

Sally did not know at this time what he and his wife's game was, but she did not care. It was Mary that had fed to her the information that she needed for the first encounter, but she still did not know how they were able to arrange for the window to fly open during the séance. She figured that Thomas was somehow responsible but not sure how he did it. Thomas and Mary had spoken at length with Doctor James and Jessica Cribbs on several occasions and were well versed on his friend Curtis from his medical school days, not only his antics but his personality. Mary had pretty much made up the story about her sister Missy and Missy's husband. The story was quite clever and much to Sally's liking especially since Sally was a strong believer and advocate for the women's rights movement that was

29

building momentum. She liked the revenge part of the story and the part where Missy escaped eternal damnation for the act of poisoning her abusive husband.

Chapter Six

Ginny received the news on Monday that she had made the cheerleading squad and was beside herself with excitement. The news was announced over the intercom system during home room so that everyone, or at least everyone that was actually listening, heard the news. You could hear shrieking throughout the building for several minutes while girlfriends of the elected elite congratulated their friends. Ginny could not wait to let her mother know the good news. *Maybe mom was right*, she thought as a wave of exuberance rushed over her. *If this can happen to me it could be the start of a change for everything, including my grades!*

Collin also heard the announcement. He too was elated but he did not shriek. However, he did make a sound, one that could barely be heard by anyone except for himself. That sound was, "Yes!" as he clenched his right hand when he heard Ginny's name called out. Collin Denton Smith, C. D. for short, was now a junior. He knew Ginny from around school. He was drawn to her subtle beauty and by what he saw was a good natured friendliness. The previous year at school, even though he at the time was a sophomore and she a freshman, they had been in one class together. That class had been chorus and they had several times said hello to each other when they saw each other outside of class. Besides being drawn to her looks and her friendliness, he loved her voice. Her words would come out slowly and sweetly and were a melody to his ears. Was he smitten? The answer to that would be, yes! Was he too timid to ask her out? The answer to that would be a yes, too. But he did not really start thinking about asking her out until this current year, so being timid was not the only excuse. His first two years of high school he was more concerned with concentrating on doing well in school and improving his abilities in sports. He was a very good student so far and was starting quarterback on the sophomore football team. He also ran track. He was now vying for the starting varsity quarterback position after a not too stellar sophomore season. The cause of that not too stellar season, he felt, was a lack of arm strength, so his passing statistics were mediocre. This, in addition to the poorly performing offensive line left him with rushed throws and being sacked much too frequently. During the summer he had concentrated on increasing his upper body strength and throwing accuracy. He had attended two football camps and started to do more in the way of weight lifting—all this to improve his chances to be starting varsity quarterback.

Anyway, with the announcement, Collin had suddenly been reminded of Ginny. His confidence scholastically and what he felt was an immense improvement physically had boosted his self-esteem and now he hoped that somehow this would also improve his confidence in dealing with the opposite sex. *I am going to congratulate her on being chosen as a cheerleader the next time I see her,* he thought. *That should remind her that I am still here at school and hopefully lead to more later,* he mused, but not certain what the 'more' would end up being. He knew that he'd eventually like to ask her out and perhaps that could be the Homecoming dance in October. He thought to himself, *I now have two goals, starting quarterback and asking Ginny to Homecoming.*

***

Ginny arrived home after attending a brief get acquainted meeting with the other sophomore cheerleaders and the cheerleading coach.

"You are home later than usual honey, any problems?"

"No problems at all, mom." And then she excitedly screamed as she started jumping up and down, "I made the cheerleading squad!" She then hugged her mom as she said, "Thanks for making this happen!"

"You made it happen, not me. How did I make it happen?

"You made it all possible by getting dad to agree, so you made it happen!"

"It would never have happened if you were not capable. Congratulations, I am so happy for you! Just remember not to get behind in your school work. Budget your time and keep organized."

"I will, I will," said Ginny while thinking *"I can do this. I've got to do this. Can I do this? I'll get Brian to help me."*

***

Collin arrived home after attending an extended practice. Since he had maintained good conditioning the extra work didn't bother him. He was hungry though. His mother and father had discovered that ever since he started the workouts the past summer his appetite had increased tremendously. "Your dad is going to have to get a second job just to be able to feed you," his mother joked. "I would've had to buy you brand-new shirts and pants too, if it weren't for the fact that you normally wear those larger sizes that make it seem like two of you can fit into them. At least you have now filled them out with your increased bulk."

"Any word on who the starting quarterback is going to be, Collin?" his dad asked.

"We will know before practice this Thursday and whoever it will be will get the majority of the reps in preparation for this weekend's game."

"I sure do hope that the coach picks you, Collin. I know you've been working so hard." his mother said.

Collin changed the subject by asking, "Hey mom, dad, do you mind if I ask a girl out to go to the Homecoming dance?"

His dad answered with, "I do not see why not. Just make sure that a girl doesn't get in the way of your goals of continuing to get good grades and doing well in your sports."

"I didn't say that I was marrying her, dad!"

Collin's dad slapped him on the back and chuckled. His mother was more interested in who the girl was, if she was cute, and how long he knew her.

"Do you have a picture of her," said his mom. "I want to see her."

Collin responded, "I suppose her picture should be in last year's yearbook. Let me go see." He returned a short while later with the yearbook. "Let's see . . . Here it is."

"Oh, she is cute. How tall is she?"

"I don't know, ma, maybe about five–four. Why?"

"I just wouldn't think it would be right if she were taller than you, that's all. It wouldn't look right in pictures."

"Mom, I haven't even asked her out yet. How do you even know if she'll say yes?"

"I don't, but this is just so much fun. My boy asking a girl out on his first real date."

"I think you will be more disappointed than me if she says no, and you've never even met her!"

His father laughed both at his son's comment and his wife's bubbliness. "I don't think I have seen your mother this happy since you got potty trained!" They all laughed.

"When is Homecoming?" his mother asked.

"In about five weeks," answered Collin.

"Well with a girl that cute you had better not dilly dally or else she may be asked by someone else!"

"I don't see her every day for any length of time. I might see her as we pass in the halls sometimes, and that's it."

"Oh, you don't have any of the same classes?" asked his mother.

"No, not this year. Last year we had one class together, but none this year."

"She must have made a big impression on you last year. What was it?" his father asked.

"Well, like mom said, she is cute. She also has a great smile and from what I saw last year she appeared to be fun to be around."

"Just remember that life is not all fun and games," his father said reminding him of his earlier admonition.

His mom added, "I admit that your dad is right but sometimes he can be such a kill–joy!"

Collin had gone to his room to get some of his homework done and to think about how he was going to find the moment to ask Ginny to the Homecoming dance, especially since he didn't see her routinely in the halls. Even if he did there certainly wasn't enough time to ask a girl out on a first date. *Let's see, I could text her. But, I don't have her phone number. Heck I don't even know if she has a cell phone. I could ask one of her friends what her number is. No, that would be too impersonal to ask her through a text. I've got it. All I need to do is find out when her cheerleading practice is done. Heck that probably isn't going to work either. I have to be on the practice field as quickly as I can right after school. There isn't going to be time to go looking for her.*

"Time for dinner," his mother yelled up to him.

"Okay, mom, I'll be right down." *I'll think of something,* he said to himself.

Collin had a good night's rest and awoke with a new idea. He knew where Ginny's locker was. He would put a note in her locker large enough so that she had to see it. *Maybe I should write it on bright colored paper too,* he thought to himself. *I can't take a chance that she won't see it. Who knows how messy of a locker she has? Maybe a little after shave? Ah, that will do it. If she doesn't see it she'll smell it!* At breakfast he told his mother his plan. His dad had already left for his commute to work. Collin said to his mom, "But I don't have any after shave. Can I use some of dad's?"

"I don't see why not, Collin. I'll get you some. You go ahead and write your note." By the time his mother came back he was packing his backpack. She said "I had to try three different scents to get you the right one. Here," she said as she handed him the bottle.

"There, that should do," he said after splashing some on.

"There is going to be no missing that, Collin," his mother said, raising her eyebrows.

"What? Did I put too much on?"

"It'll be alright," said his mother.

When Collin got to school he went straight to his locker to make sure that he had all the text books needed for the first three classes since he would not be near his locker again until after his third class. The locker next to him belonged to his friend Nick. Nick was on the football team too and when he got to his locker he caught a whiff of the after shave that Collin had placed on the note and he said "Whew, do I smell a skunk?"

"What the hell are you talking about, Nick?"

"Well I smell something and it ain't me, so it's got to be you!"

"I thought it smelled pretty good," Collin said.

"Don't mind me," answered Nick. "It doesn't smell that bad but what are you doing with smell–good on? Do you think you have been nominated for the Heisman or something?"

Becoming more concerned that he had overdone it with the after shave, Collin answered. "No I don't think I have been nominated for the Heisman. I'm trying to get a note to a girl that I want to ask to Homecoming but I rarely see her anymore this year. She is a sophomore in case you want to know, and no, I don't know her phone number or her email address. That should cover it. End of conversation until mission accomplished. If I'm successful I will fill you in."

"Boy, talk about taking charge! Next I'll bet that you will want to run the offense with your own play calling. Couldn't you have clued me in about this?"

Collin, now rushing, for he knew he only had a couple of minutes to get to class, said to Nick, "What for? My mind is set on this."

"Good luck, Romeo!" Nick said as Collin walked quickly away down the hall.

As he walked he started to think about when he could place the note in Ginny's locker. He knew where her locker was because he had seen her one day busily rummaging through it. He hadn't had time to stop and say hello and she looked too busy at the time. Anyway, his second and third period classes were very close to each other, so he figured he could make a trip between classes and drop the note in her locker since it was close enough for him to do it without being late for third period.

***

End of second period, good, Collin said to himself. He knew he didn't have to rush since he had plenty of time to get to her locker. No sooner had he gone down the stairs to the first floor than he encountered Ginny who was about to go up the stairs. Collin smiled and said, "Ginny! Hello! Good to see you!"

Taken by surprise, Ginny looked back to see who greeted her. "Oh, hello Collin," she said as she smiled back. "How are you? It's nice to see you too." She continued on up the stairs as Collin briefly followed her with his eyes. He then proceeded to her locker and placed the note through a gap in the door.

The next time Ginny got back to her locker was a couple of hours later. By that time anyone that went past her locker could smell the after shave. She thought that the fragrance must be coming from someone else's locker nearby but when she opened her locker there was no doubt as to where it was coming from. Neither could she miss the bright green fluorescent folded paper lying on top of her stack of books. She was almost afraid to touch it but was too curious. She didn't have time to read it so she tucked it into one of her books and sped off to lunch.

No sooner than she got to the lunch line than Jenny, one of her friends, leaned over to her and said, "You must have a man living in your locker? A rather mature man from the scent of it!" Jenny was smiling from ear to ear.

When Ginny got to the lunch table she said, "What are you talking about?"

"Oh, you aren't going to act like you don't know? I can still smell it all around you."

"I really don't know. I stopped by my locker before lunch and I found a note but I didn't get a chance to read it."

"So, okay, you've got the time now. Let's look at it!" Ginny pulled out the fluorescent green note from her biology book. "Boy, how much cologne did he put on that?" Jenny said as she acted like she couldn't catch her breath.

"Please stop making such a scene," Ginny whispered tersely, trying not to garner any attention in their direction. "I'm going to read it myself first. So don't try to peek, Jenny."

Jenny sat back with a pouty face and said, "Oh, come on, what fun is that?"

Unfolding the note Ginny read, *Ginny, I was in your chorus class last year. My name is Collin Smith. I used to say hi to you when we were in class. I would like to talk to you, but we don't have any classes together this year. Would you please either text me at 779‒337‒9327 or email me at cds@haremail.net? I want to ask you something important and, by the way, congratulations on being named to the cheerleading squad!* She folded the note back up and put it in a pocket of her jeans.

"C'mon, aren't you going to tell me who it was from? And what did he say? It was a him, wasn't it? Or was it the maintenance man? I see how he looks at you. Oh, that would be sick!"

"Can you please stop, Jen? And catch your breath." Once Jenny calmed down Ginny told her his name.

"Are you serious, Ginny?"

"Yes, I am serious. What is the big deal?"

"Heck, you are a cheerleader and you don't know that he is possibly going to be the starting varsity quarterback?"

Wide-eyed, Ginny shrieked, "Are you serious? No, I didn't know that!"

"So, why did he send you the note, Ginny?"

"He just said that he wanted me to contact him since he didn't know how to reach me and that he wanted to ask me something important."

"Ask you something important. Is that it? Really, that's all! You didn't tell me everything, did you? Alright, spill it all."

"No, really, that's basically all it said."

"You are going to call him, right? I've got to be there when you call him. When are you going to call him?"

"Will you stop? I am not going to call him."

"What do you mean you are not going to call him?"

"You know that I don't have my own phone because my dad thinks that I'd be on the phone instead of studying. You know how he is about that. So, I was going to send him an email."

"An email! How impersonal is that? Wouldn't you rather talk to him, hear his voice? Damn, I'll let you use my cell phone, okay?"

"Okay, but when? I already told you that my dad is a 'study Nazi'. He expects me home right after cheerleading practice. How am I going to do this?"

"He doesn't make you study all weekend, does he?"

"No."

"Then you come to my house for a sleep–over on Friday night and we'll call Collin then. He probably is going to have a curfew before the game on Saturday so we shouldn't have a problem getting ahold of him."

"Okay, I'll ask my mother if I can come over on Friday. We can go straight to the sophomore game from your house on Saturday and then stay for the varsity game."

"Okay, game on!" exclaimed Jenny.

***

Ginny could not wait until Friday to call Collin. She couldn't imagine what he wanted to talk about but he said it was important. She did not realize that her putting off the call until Friday was going to cause Collin to wonder what was going on.

And he did wonder. He wondered if she had even gotten the note and he started to think to himself. How could she have not gotten the note? The after shave and the color had to make her see it! She had to have seen it! Maybe she's just blowing me off. Why would she do that? Stop thinking that way. There must be a good explanation. He was having a hard time thinking about anything else. But he knew that he had to refocus his concentration since he had just found out on Thursday that he was going to be the starting quarterback on Saturday! He knew that doing well could mean having the starting position for the entire season.

Ginny was wrapped up with her cheerleading practice and was trying to keep up with her studies. She had been receiving help from her brother, Brian, as he had promised, and she felt that she was making some progress. She knew that her brother's help was vital and her mother did say that sometimes when having more, not less, on your schedule helped to budget your time and concentrate better. Whatever it was, it seemed to be working, although she still didn't like that she had to study so much.

Ginny had begged her mother to give her permission to spend Friday night at Jen's house and then go to the games on Saturday. Her mother had already seen a change in Ginny at home since she began cheerleading practice and she'd given her the okay for the sleepover.

***

"We worked extra hard on some tumbling moves today with our cheers, Jen. I think we're ready to go tomorrow," Ginny said as they walked to Jenny's house on Friday evening.

"Is that all you can talk about? How about the phone call? Did you forget about that?"

"No, I haven't forgotten. I am more than a little nervous though about calling him. What if I say something stupid?"

"Don't be silly. He's just the starting varsity quarterback."

"Yes, I know that. Don't make this any harder for me. What is so important that he wants to talk to me?"

"Maybe he is sweet on you!" Jenny said in a sugary sweet tone.

"Oh stop! That note had no hint of sweetness. It was pretty matter of fact."

"You never know", Jenny said slowly as she drew out each word.

42

After dinner, Ginny and Jenny went to Jenny's bedroom where Ginny called Collin. Collin had just finished dinner and was relaxing on his bed before going over his playbook one more time before the next day's game. He answered the phone on the third ring. "Hello," he said.

"Hello, this is Ginny Chandler. Is this Collin?"

Collin sprang up to a seated position and said, "It sure is. So you did get my note?" He was going to say, *I've been waiting four days for your call,* but he stopped the impulse and said to himself, *you can't do that dummy. Don't sound stupid and desperate.* So he waited for her answer.

"Yes, I got your note. How was I to miss it? But what is so important?"

Jenny was thinking, *that's her—right to the point*!

Collin answered without nervousness because he had been rehearsing, "I'd like to take you to the Homecoming dance. Do you want to go?"

Ginny was stunned. She had been wanting to go but thought that perhaps one of the boys that she knew in her own class would end up asking her. Jenny blurted, "What did he say. What did he say?" as Ginny was gesturing for her to shut up so that she could hear if Collin was saying anything else.

"I'm sorry, did you say something else?"

"Besides what?" Collin asked.

"Besides asking me to go to Homecoming with you."

"No, that was it. So would you like to go?"

"You surprised me," said Ginny and then added, "Not that this isn't important but it's a different kind of important. Anyway, I need to ask my parents if I can."

"So, when can you get back to me?" continued Collin.

"Why don't you call me next Wednesday? You have my number now."

"That's not your number! That's my number!" Jenny barked aggressively but quietly and with some agitation.

"On second thought I will email you on Wednesday to let you know. You gave me your email address."

"Why so long?" asked Collin.

"A girl has to think about these things," replied Ginny with a smile on her face and a roll of her eyes.

"A girl has to think about these things?" Oh my God, what kind of comment was that?" Jenny said as she too rolled her eyes. "I can't believe you just said that!"

"I mean, I do have to ask my parents."

"I know, you told me that," Collin replied mildly confused.

"So, anyway, I will email you my answer on Wednesday. Oh, and thanks for the congratulations. Congratulations to you, too, on being named starting quarterback. That is pretty impressive."

"Now you're revving up," quipped Jenny so only Ginny could hear her.

"Are you excited?" Ginny asked Collin.

"I am a little anxious, especially since I beat out the starter from last year. I want to do well and of course we want to win. Hey, I've got to get going. I need to finish reviewing my playbook before I hit the sack. Goodnight, and I will be looking forward to your answer. I hope you can go."

"Bye," answered Ginny.

At the end of the call Jenny commented, "That started out weak but you ended strong; good strong ending comments.

I'd have to rate that a 6.5 out of 10 with a difficulty scale of 2.3!"

"What's that all about?" Ginny asked.

"Don't mind me. I've got Sochi on my mind."

"Huh?" Ginny replied.

"You know, Sochi, the Winter Olympics?"

Ginny sat down next to Jenny's bed and said to Jenny, "How am I going to get my parents to let me go? I've just gotten my dad, against all odds, to let me go out for cheerleading and then my mom got him to let me come here this weekend. I'm going to be pushing my luck expecting him to allow this!"

"Challenges are good for the soul, Gin."

Ginny had an idea. She was going to ask Brian for help after she told her mom about being asked to the dance. She thought that Brian, the excellent student that he was, could explain to their dad how hard she had been trying and that he, Brian, had seen progress in her work. She knew her mother would be supportive.

**

"Honey, we saw you at the football game. You did great and it looked like you were having a blast," Rose said with the utmost sincerity.

"You were there? And you got dad to come?"

"Yes, it was his Saturday off from work and I asked him on a date!"

"Where is he now?" Ginny asked.

"He went to the hardware store to get some light bulbs."

"Did he just leave?"

"Just a few minutes ago. Why?"

Ginny was getting excited about telling her mom about being asked to Homecoming and she wanted get it done before her dad returned home. "I was asked by the varsity quarterback to go to Homecoming! Can I go? Can I go?"

"Whoa!" said her mom. "I don't care if he is the President of the United States! I don't know him. How long have you known him?"

"I was surprised that he asked me. I only said hi to him one time last year during chorus."

"You only said hi one time and he asked you out?"

"Well, we probably said hi more than half of the semester, but only hi or hello."

"Only hi or hello! So, you really don't know anything about him. That is, besides his being the varsity quarterback."

"He seemed very nice in class! I mean, he didn't seem all into himself . . . And he's cute!"

"I'll have to discuss this with your dad, and you know that this is not going to be an easy sell. Plus, I'll need to know more, like how is he doing in school and has he caused any trouble, in school or out. And, what is his name?"

"His name is Collin Smith and how am I going to find out all that information?"

Her mother responded, "Come on, I'm sure that you can find someone in your school that can get you that information. The sooner you get that information for me the sooner I'll be able to ask your dad for his okay. But I'll only ask him if I approve of Collin first. And that is my final word."

***

Ginny knew who to turn to and that was Jenny. She seemed to be on top of everything around school.

"Jenny, you have got to help me out!"

"From the sound of you it sounds like you're going to owe me. What is it?"

"I need to find out more about Collin before my mom will even talk to my dad about letting me go with him."

"Like what?"

"Like I need to know something about his grades and whether he has been in or caused any trouble."

"I don't know. That sounds like it could be difficult, but . . . I'll see what I can do."

"Remember that I have to get back to Collin by Wednesday!"

"Wednesday, Shmendsday. He can wait a little bit longer if necessary."

"What if he asks someone else if I don't answer by Wednesday?"

"What makes you think he would do that? You really do not know him at all, do you? Think about it! He asked you, a sophomore! Don't you think he could have asked any girl and they would have jumped at the chance to go with him? If you don't get your answer from your parents by Wednesday, let him know you need more time."

Remarkably on Wednesday morning Jenny had the information that Ginny needed. Collin was a B−plus to A student and had not been in trouble except for getting *timed out* from the park district swimming pool for dunking a friend the past summer.

"He's a model citizen," reported Jenny.

"Where and how did you get this information so fast?" asked Ginny.

"I have my sources."

"C'mon, my mom isn't going to just buy this!"

"I really can't tell you Gin. I may get my source in trouble. Just try telling your mom and see what she says. If she accepts it without asking how you got the information you're home free. If not, we'll worry about that then."

Chapter Seven

August and Beverly Frederick had arrived before anyone else, so they had time for some conversation with the doctor and his wife. Beverly and Jessica stayed in the front room while the men went into the parlor.

"Jessica, whatever is cooking smells absolutely delicious," said Beverly.

"I wish that I could tell you what it is but I really don't know. Although, I do guarantee that you will enjoy it! As you know from the first time you were here, we have a wonderful cook."

"We did not get to talk too much the last time, Jessica. Do you do much work around your house or does Bessie do a lot for you?"

"Work in the house? Heavens no, I do not do any of that. I am beyond that. I am very much involved in charity work for the disabled and the poor and have been working very hard promoting women's rights."

"I have had some thoughts of joining a group that helps the disabled through my church. Is that how you got involved, Jessica?"

"You can call me Jess, dear Beverly, and yes I did get started through my church, but . . ."

"But what?" asked Beverly.

"I am not sure you should hear the rest because it is only suspicion, but a rather strong suspicion. I am concerned of

49

starting a rumor, since I do not know this for certain, so keep it to yourself. Many of us in my group were suspicious that the pastor would use part of the monies that we earned for the poor on himself. I could not tolerate that and so I decided to leave the group. Now, I do the same thing with another group of women which is not tied to the church."

"That is quite horrible about the reverend," said Beverly.

"Yes, and that is when I started to get interested in women's equality issues also. It seemed to me that there was, and still is, a double standard for men and for women which I do not believe is right, and many others, both women and men, feel the same way. Women are expected to stay at home and be the moral compass for the home, but men can get away with anything including infidelity. I must say that I was influenced by what Elizabeth Stanton and Susan Anthony were saying and decided to go hear them speak. Since then I've been submitting opinions to the paper which occasionally they'll print concerning women's rights, including the right to keep one's wages, the right to divorce and the right to vote. It's just unfortunate that I must keep the opinions anonymous to protect my husband from any backlash."

"Oh my Lord! And your husband is alright with that? I never would have thought . . ."

"Oh yes, he is perfectly fine with what I do as long as it remains anonymous until women's rights become commonly accepted. He believes wholeheartedly in a woman's ability to take care of herself and have the same rights as men do. I am somewhat surprised he has not talked to you about this since you assist him with his work."

"Oh, he does often say when he sees a married woman with scars on her arms, legs, or back that he knows they are probably from a beating given to her by her husband. He does seem upset, but we go about taking care of her wounds and not making judgments."

"I will tell you a secret Beverly, he does make judgments, and the judgment is not for the husband and the acceptance of this type of abuse. He comes home in such a mood sometimes that I know that he has been bothered by something."

"Why does he not say anything, Jess?"

"It is not in his best interest to say something. As I mentioned, it is accepted for a husband to do that to his wife if they feel they are justified in doing so."

The Cribbs' and Fredericks' conversation was interrupted by the remaining couples who happened to arrive at the front door simultaneously.

Bessie answered the door and Dr. and Mrs. Cribbs greeted each couple as they came in. The Fredericks also extended their greetings as Bessie went off to hang up the hats and coats. August went on to say, "I am so glad that we are all able to get together again. Beverly and I had such a wonderful time the last occasion we got together."

More time was spent with dinner conversation that evening, and as usual Mary Kent was hanging on to everything she could hear. Dr. Cribbs started the conversation by asking everyone to tell the others what it was that they did for a living. Samuel Ulrich didn't hesitate and said that he was a pharmacist and pitched, "Please get all your medicines from the Ulrich Apothecary; best prices in town and discounts to all of you!"

Elsa followed saying, "I teach at Philos Seminary–teaching boys from ages 6 through 9 . . ." She also added impulsively, and rather uncharacteristically and boldly for her, ". . . and I wish that I had girls to teach also."

Mr. Kent, taken a bit aback by Elsa's bold statement asked her, "And do you have more to add to that statement?"

"Yes," and with a stern voice and a scowl on her face as if she were trying to gain order in her classroom she said, "Yes, it is about time that girls are given the same opportunities to learn more than the basics!" Samuel was surprised to hear Elsa speak this way in a mixed gathering. It is not that he did not know her view. He was coming around to share that view but this was a new Elsa that was now speaking openly about the issue.

Thomas Kent, reacting to Elsa's new-found confidence, asked Elsa for permission to speak. "Dear Elsa, if you are finished, might I have your kind permission to speak?" He truly was not trying to make fun of her, but several at the table took it as if he were attempting to act like one of her students—as if he were asking permission to do something, and they laughed.

Elsa blushed as she thought about how she must have sounded, and then she laughed and said, "I may have gotten carried away, but it is true!" She added, "And yes, you have my permission to speak, Mr. Kent." Additional laughter from everyone followed Elsa's remark.

Thomas stated that he was in banking. He actually stated, "I am banking on your letting me make more money for you if you invest with me." Everyone in the room sighed at the pun except his wife who jabbed him in the side and said, "Really Thomas?" He then added, "Yes really," and then paused briefly to look at Mary, his wife. He went on to say, "And any money that I earn for you would be money in the bank." That earned him another jab in the side and laughter from the men.

Mary continued the occupational round and said that she had the responsibility to make their home always immaculate so as to present a beautiful place for her husband's clients to visit. She added that her job was to be the custodian of her husband's financial well–being. Seizing the opportunity opened by what Jessica and Elsa had related earlier she stated that she was also involved in promoting for women's rights and specifically the right to choose how they wished to spend their lives, whether it be working outside the home like men do or staying home to take care of their families. She made a point of adding–only if they decide to have a family. She stopped short of adding a right for a woman to decide whether to be able to choose to have her unborn child aborted for she was not certain as yet as to how the group would receive it, although she knew that there were many women already who sought potions for prevention of pregnancy and even resorted to abortionists. When it came to the Hughses, everyone already knew that they both worked to publish *The Herald*, a newspaper which enjoyed a wide circulation and was well respected. What people were not aware of was that they also published a smaller paper that made most of its revenue from running ads for a wide variety of things including the potions and abortive services that Mary Kent knew were available. Dr. Cribbs had no need to announce what he did but his wife stated that she was the wife of the esteemed Dr. Cribbs and liked it that way since it gave her the opportunity to do charitable work and work on causes and issues she felt were important. Beverly had already learned what those causes and issues were but Sarah was not aware and she was quite interested. "What issues are you interested in, Jessica?"

"I'd love to discuss that with you and perhaps we can do that after Miss Cooke brings us in touch with those we want to reach tonight. But, we haven't yet heard from Mr. Fredericks and his wife," added Jessica Cribbs.

August seized the moment and said, "Some of you know what I do and some of you do not, but here is a hint," as he said in a clear and robust voice, "I have for all of you, tickets. I would take pleasure in having you attend the inaugural performance of *Our American Cousin* at the Crown Theater in one week's time." And then he bowed. Everyone looked at each other quizzically.

His wife, Beverly, seeing their questioning gazes said, "He has the lead in the play." They all clapped their hands and indicated their pleasure at his invitation and their willingness to attend. Much conversation continued throughout dinner and Mary had much to pay attention to. Whenever possible she tried to steer conversation to family, past and present.

Mary was pleasantly, but not totally surprised of Jessica Cribbs' interest in women's rights. She suspected that the Cribbses were somewhat older than the remainder of the group but were open minded and willing to adapt a more progressive attitude as seen by their acceptance of Spiritism. Mary certainly wanted to know if Jessica sided with her on social issues and was interested to hear what Jessica had to say about her interests after Miss Cooke was done for the evening. She knew the importance of knowing who were your friends–those you could trust, and those whom you could not!

They all next retired to the parlor. As on the first occasion, a fire was burning for warmth and candles were again lit around the room to create subdued light so as to encourage quiet and concentration. Sally Cooke gave instructions again on the importance of concentrating on each one's now deceased person of interest so as to encourage their spirit presence. Soon after saying this, Sally indicated that she was picking up what she felt was a significant amount of psychic energy.

"I can feel some tingling in my fingertips," she said.

Quickly her irises flipped upward revealing only the whites of her eyes and her head fell forward hiding her face. Elsa and Sarah let out a high – pitched shriek as Beverly

Fredericks shouted, "I think she is having a seizure?" No sooner had she said this than her head was straight up again, but her gaze was as if she were looking straight through the opposite wall. It was only the Cribbses and the Kents that were able to maintain their concentration during what was a disconcerting passage of events for the others. It started to get colder and darker in the room. Elsa and Samuel, who were sitting facing the fireplace, could see that the flames in the fireplace had reduced to a flicker. Sally's face contorted and at of one corner of her mouth there appeared to be some type of liquid. Beverly saw this and said to August quietly, "Look, she's drooling now. She must be having a seizure!" Beverly wanted to get up and give Sally some assistance but August restrained her. The liquid coming from Sally's mouth continued for several minutes. It ran down her face and dripped off her chin and collected on the table beneath Sally's left hand and Mary's right. The liquid was sticky and Mary found that she could not easily move her arm or hand that was grasping Sally's. Samuel could feel Elsa's grip around his arm getting tighter, so he put his arm around her and said, "Remember that the spirits are not here to hurt us." Elsa refused to loosen her grip. She would have been out the door already but she did not know what was safer, staying or leaving. Seeing that the ooze was slowing down she relaxed just a bit, but then there was a voice. No one at the table could identify it. The voice said, "I have been summoned to tell you this—Women should not lose hope for great strides in fairness will occur for them. Soon you will see women able to divorce their husbands for beating them. Soon you will see girls able to obtain an education equal to that of boys. There is much more that will happen and these things will come to pass. It is best not to resist otherwise time and progress will pass you by." Everyone at the table, except for Sally who was in her trance, murmured that they had no idea who was speaking. Mary spoke out saying, "Who are you, spirit? We are not familiar with who you are?" The voice said, "I represent all the spirits of women who have been abused and whose rights have been withheld from them." With that, Sally shook her head from side to side and her eyes came back to normal. She and Mary tried to pick up their hands that had been covered by the ooze but found that they could not. As they all gathered to try to help release what had ensnared the two women's hands, Samuel saw something in the fireplace. He walked closer and discovered the same substance that had ensnared the women's hands. "This is quite interesting," he said. "It appears as though the substance binding your hands to the table is present here on the hearth." Sally said, "The spirit must have entered your home, Dr. Cribbs, through the chimney. I have heard of this type of substance being left by the visit of a spirit or spirits, but this is the first time it has happened for me! Whomever the spirit was must have been powerful to be able to do this. Who conjured up this spirit?" They all tried to answer at the same time creating an unintelligible babble. August finally spoke collectively for the group, saying, "It appears as though no one can identify the voice and we must assume that somehow our concentrating came to no avail in contacting who we were individually trying to reach."

Mary finally said, "The spirit said that she was speaking for all women whose rights and opportunities have been withheld, and for those that have been abused. I also believe she was telling us that these abuses will change and women will gain their rights, and if we resist this change we will be left in the past with no hope in the future."

Sally proposed that perhaps all the discussion during dinner about rights for women may have opened up a portal for this spirit to enter. She then said, "I could sense deep emotions being shared during dinner. This spirit, who obviously had an important message to deliver, was able to pick up on the vibrations generated by your emotions."

Thomas Kent, who knew what was going on, played along with the ruse and argued that what the spirit said could mean many different things to different people. Mary Kent argued back, saying that it was clear that the spirit was announcing the end to women's subjugation. This started a vigorous discussion which revealed the thoughts of everyone regarding these issues.

Being wrapped–up in their discussion they almost forgot about Sally and Mary and their inability to free their hands from being secured to the table by the sticky jelly–like ooze. Jessica called out to Bessie to get some soap and water to wash the ooze off but it wouldn't budge. It finally took vinegar to loosen the substance to a more fluid consistency at which point it could be wiped easily away. As they did this they continued their spirited discussion, finding in the end that they agreed on many of the same things. Mary, not hearing any discussion related to sexual proclivities, decided not to chance the topic, at least not yet.

Jessica Cribbs summed it up when she said, "Sarah, the spirit spoke of what I have been working on for years and it sounds like we all have similar thoughts on these issues!"

Sally exhaled an enormous sigh of relief to find that her ploy worked out much better than she had imagined. It appeared that they had all bought into her act. She was pleased that they had seemed to enjoy each other's company, and she felt if she played her cards right, she might even be able to garner even more for her performances. Mary couldn't have been happier either.

Chapter Eight

It was already Wednesday evening and Ginny was only now letting her mother know what she had found out about her possible future date. She and her mother were finishing cleaning up after dinner. Her father had gone to take a shower.

Ginny said to her mom, "I have the information you want about Collin."

"Okay."

"He is a 'B–plus' student and he is not a troublemaker."

"And where did you get that information?"

"I got it from a reliable source."

"And that would be?"

Ginny thought on her feet and said, "From one of the people that work in the school office. My friend Jenny knows her and she told Jenny that there was nothing to worry about with Collin."

Rose thought for a brief second and then said, "Okay, I will talk to your father. He seemed in a good mood today at dinner. By the way, how have you been doing on homework and quizzes?"

"Since Brian has been helping me I am doing better. The homework seems to be getting easier and I had 'B's' on math and biology quizzes this past week."

"That will help, and I know that your father is going to ask before he's going to give any permission."

While watching the evening news together Rose mentioned to Alex what Ginny had told her about her quiz grades the past week, and that homework was not as much of a problem as it had been. She told him that working with Brian was probably helping her. She also said that perhaps the cheerleading was helping her self-confidence. "I'm glad to hear that," he said, and added, "I don't need to tell you how important that I feel an education is."

"Yes, you know that I know that. I would like to not have to work doing hair and nails every day, then work weekends too, to give our kids what we feel they need. I know that I could have been able to earn better if I went to college. But it is not what I did and I'm okay with it. I found the man that I love and we have three wonderful children. They are all different, and I love them all, and I know you do to."

"Yes, I do, but I also want each of them not to miss their chance for a higher education." Alex's attention became fixed to the TV. "Hold on. I want to listen to this." The reporter announced that a secret deal had just been concluded with the Iranian government to withdraw the majority of economic sanctions in exchange for not increasing their level of nuclear enrichment and refraining from converting to weapons–grade level. "What do these morons think they're doing trusting these guys?" Alex fumed with great consternation.

Rose could tell that this was not the time to pursue asking him his permission for Ginny's request. She said, "I'm getting tired. That's it for me." She closed her eyes, turned to her side and just thought, *how dare that international politics play havoc with my domestic policy!*

Before Ginny left for school the next morning she asked her mother whether she had asked her dad about Homecoming.

Rose said to her that it was not a good time last night due to political issues and then said, "You better get going or you will be late for school." Ginny ran out the door wondering what her mother was talking about–*political issues.*

Jenny met Ginny at her locker and asked, "Any answer yet from your parents?"

Ginny answered, "No, my mom said that there was something about politics and it wasn't a good time."

"What was that all about," Jenny asked.

"You think I have any clue? Heck, it is Thursday now, and I still don't have an answer!"

"How long do you think it will be?"

"Who's sounding nervous now, Jenny? I thought you said that I had nothing to worry about if it took me longer than Wednesday to find out!"

"Oh, no, I think you will still be okay. Did you let him know?"

"Collin? No, I only found this out this morning just before I left the house. I'll have to let him know tonight that it is going to take longer. I hope that he doesn't ask someone else."

Jenny said, "Here, let's send him a text now before homeroom." *Collin, I need a bit more time before I can let you know if I can go to Homecoming with you. My mother has not had a chance to ask my father about it yet.* "There, that should do it, nice, but matter of fact. It's enough to show your interest, but not so much to show you're anxious as hell that he'll ask someone else and leave you sitting at home."

"Stop it, Jenny. You know this is nerve wracking!"

At the same time, Nick asked Collin, "Did you ever get an answer from that girl you were going to ask out to Homecoming?"

Collin, somewhat perturbed, responded, "No, she said she would get back to me by yesterday and I haven't heard anything!"

"Good luck. She is just playing around with you, I'm sure. That's what girls do. See you later my man. I've got to get going."

"Talk to you later, Nick." Collin then received the text message from Ginny. He read it and said to himself, *Okay, just relax. Be patient.*

***

It was now Saturday and Rose still did not have a chance to bring up the question of Homecoming to Alex. It was Alex's Saturday to work, so he wouldn't be home until later that afternoon. She would try to ask him when he got home, as long as he didn't have too hard of a day at work.

Alex came home and was in a very good mood. He was in a good mood because during the day both Rose and Alex had been told by their son, Brian, that he had been offered full–ride academic scholarships from both Stanford University and Yale. He came in saying, "Where is Brian?"

"Up in his room," answered Rose.

Alex ran up the stairs and knocked on Brian's door before walking in. Brian had barely gotten up from his chair before Alex was in his room throwing his arms around him and hugging him and saying a loud "CONGRATULATIONS SON!"

Marty and Ginny were at home and came to see what was going on. "Congratulations for what?" both Ginny and Marty said at the same time.

"Congratulations for what! Don't you know that your brother received full–ride scholarships from both Stanford and Yale? Marty wasn't really sure what that meant but Ginny did. She was glad to see her father happy, but concerned that it might put even more pressure on her to match her brother's elite standard.

Ginny did finally say, "I am so happy for you Brian! Congratulations!" And then a sense of panic welled up in her as she thought, *if he is so far away at school, how is he going to be able to help me next year with my studies?*

Alex announced, "We are all going out tonight for a celebration."

"Honey, but I have to work tonight, remember?"

"Okay, tomorrow then. We'll go out for brunch."

"Where", Brian asked.

Rose answered, "How about Christies? I heard it is very nice and they have an all you can eat buffet! But, it's expensive."

Alex shrugged off Rose's last comment and said, "Christies it is. Nothing is too good for my son."

No one got up early on Sunday morning in the Chandler family since Rose usually worked late hours on Saturday night. She liked to sleep in and no one in the family was going to argue. They did however attend church services routinely at ten thirty in the morning so they generally didn't sleep past nine thirty. Alex, although he went to services, was not convinced of God's existence. He, like many of his friends, began to question God's existence while they were in their mid to late teens. When his father died, leaving him the responsibility to help his mother provide for the family, he started to doubt. He could not understand how a benevolent god could rob him of his desire to attend college, let alone his father! It didn't matter how many times or how many people told him that he was doing an honorable thing, or that God had other plans for him, he was not convinced. But Rose got him to attend church again. His going with her made her happy. And he was often surprised when he found the words of a sermon having meaning for him.

While getting dressed for church services Rose told Alex that Ginny had started to improve her performance at school and that she had received B's on two quizzes over the past week. He refrained from saying that she could then move on to A's and commented that that was good to hear.

"I knew that she had it in her," he said. Then Rose went on to say that Ginny was asked to the Homecoming dance. She held off in saying that it was the starting quarterback for the varsity team that had asked her. She thought that he may not be endeared to the thought of some jock older than Ginny taking her out. She went on to say, "I hear he is a very good student and not a troublemaker."

She was surprised when he said to her, "That's nice to hear. When is Homecoming?" He was still on his high from Brian's news the day before and was looking forward to the all you can eat meal after the church service. His thought was to enjoy the celebration meal and then come back home and enjoy afternoon football. And if he fell asleep because he ate too much, so be it. "So, it's okay if she goes with this boy?"

"I don't see why not. It sounds like she deserves it, and from what you have said about the boy, he sounds safe enough."

Rose said to herself, *Oh God! That was too easy.*

On their way to church Rose turned around and started to whisper to Ginny, who was seated in back of her, that her father gave the okay for her to go to the Homecoming dance. Alex asked, "Okay what is this secrecy? Rose finished telling Ginny and Ginny shrieked with joy. Alex, startled, said "What's going on back there?"

"Oh, thank you so much dad for letting me go to the dance with Collin!"

"Since your mother has told me you're doing better in school I can't see why you shouldn't be able to go. But I am expecting you to not slack off!"

"I won't dad! You can count on me!" answered Ginny. She was sensing good things happening for her and she felt good that her father was starting to sound proud of her.

After the church service they went directly to Christies. It was the first time they had been there. They were seated by a hostess and she explained to them that there was a flat price for the brunch items except that desserts and alcoholic drinks were extra. She also told them that they would have a waiter for the alcohol and that they would settle the bill with him when they were done with their meal.

They were amazed at the amount and variety of the food. Not only did they have the usual eggs, bacon, sausage and juice, but much more. They had omelets made by a chef right in front of you, a panoply of baked goods, fresh shrimp, and much-much more. They had never feasted in such a manner, not even on Thanksgiving or Christmas Day!

Marty's eyes were everywhere looking at all the things he wanted to try. Brian surveyed everything and deliberately made his choices. Regardless of how they each went about it, the boys all ended up making pigs of themselves with the amount of food that they ate-even Alex. Rose and Ginny were more restrained in the amounts that they chose but did try a lot of the selections. They both gave the appearance of not eating a lot but by the time they were done they also felt stuffed. Alex even indulged in a couple of Bloody Mary's, and Rose, one Mimosa. After the meal, and before they left the restaurant, Alex commented, "We can all thank Brian for this. Well done Brian. Perhaps we can do this again, right Ginny and Marty?" Ginny and Marty knew what their father was referring to. He didn't need to say it. Marty was realistic with himself for he knew that he was not as smart as his brother, at least book smart. He knew he would have to succeed in other ways. Ginny was not sure how to succeed in any other way but she knew she had to work her tail off in order to do so, and she was not sure she had it in her. With her brother Brian going away for school next year she didn't know how she was going to do it and anxiety started to well up in her again.

Alex asked Brian to drive home because he did not want to trust his driving with the alcohol he had just consumed. He explained that to Ginny and Marty so as to make an impression on not drinking and driving. Soon they were on the road and talking about the great food they had and bragging about who ate the most sausage, the most bacon, etcetera, etcetera.

By the time they arrived home food coma had caught up with the boys and they were soon passed out on the couch. But Ginny didn't have time to waste on a nap. She still had to get in touch with Collin to tell him that she could go with him to the homecoming dance. As she started to email Collin her anxiety concerning Brian's leaving the next year started to well up in her again. She fought it off. She was determined not to let worry about the next year without Brian ruin the remainder of her current year, a year that had started to turn out better than she could have possibly hoped. She would follow Jenny's advice and not worry about problems until the time came to have to worry about them. She had proved it to herself when she was put on the spot regarding her source of information about Collin. She was quickly able to say that her information was from a reliable source because it was from someone that worked in the front office of the school. She was very proud of herself about her quick thinking.

Ginny turned on her music on her computer and plugged in her ear buds. She started singing to the music and her mother could hear her. Rose got a smile on her face as she thought about her daughter and the good things that she felt were happening in her life. Of course she was proud of Brian, but she was actually more moved and elated for Ginny because she knew Brian's capabilities. Her concern was for her daughter. Marty was still too young to worry too much about.

Ginny sent an email to Collin. *Collin, Thank you for asking me to go to Homecoming. I am sorry that I made you wait so long for my answer. I would love to go with you and my parents are okay with it. By the way, congratulations on the win this past Saturday! Ginny.*

***

Collin had been on his computer doing some research for a history assignment and saw an alert for an email message. He paused his research to look at his message and saw it was from Ginny. He first saw her words *I am sorry* and was about to freak thinking that she was not going to go with him, but he read to the end and said, "Finally!" and, "Thank God her parents are fine with it." He wrote back, *I got your message and I'm very glad that you can go with me. I'll get back to you with details. By the way, I called the number of the phone you used when you sent the text some days ago. You do need to get your own phone. Your friend was nice, but it would be nice to be able to talk to you. In the meantime, continue to email. Let me know if you get a cell. Maybe we can find a place to meet and talk sometime at school when we aren't in class. I'll attach my class schedule with my room assignments. If you take a look at it maybe you can see where we can meet during the day. Talk to you later. Collin.*

***

Ginny agreed that she needed to have a cell phone, but knew that she would be pushing it if she asked for one. *Maybe for Christmas she mused. I would probably have to have spectacular grades by the end of the semester if that were to happen.* She put off thinking about that any further since grades would not come out until after the semester break and that would be after Christmas. She knew that she should get going on her homework but she couldn't concentrate because now her thoughts were filled with what she was going to wear to the homecoming dance.

Chapter Nine

Mary had already directed the housemaids on what needed to be done for the day and set out for Fourth Avenue Tabernacle Church. She had been in contact within the past few weeks with a woman she felt could be a business partner of sorts. In order to make contact with this woman she had entrusted the Lloyd's City Post to deliver her mail. She felt that it was safe to use Lloyd's because of the company's guarantee to deliver the mail confidentially. Since they had built their reputation on this standard she felt very secure that they would not risk exposing to whom she was sending her letters.

Those letters were being received by a woman who was engaged in *restoring a woman's natural cycle or rhythm* from what the ads said in the 'penny press' papers. Mary knew what most people knew, that the ads were for abortive services without saying as much. The owners of these newspapers were more than happy to accept the fee to run these ads and then they had their gall having editorialists provide unfavorable opinions regarding these services. The letters needed secrecy because the practice of abortion was illegal and one could end up in jail. Some states had even passed the death penalty as punishment for the offense. So, Mary was not about to take any chances.

It was ten o'clock in the morning when she arrived at the church and a morning service had just ended. She walked through the large ornately carved wooden doors facing the street and entered the vestibule of the church. She took off her scarf that was bundled across her face and placed a black thickly–laced veil over her head. You could barely see the tip of her nose. She wanted to take little chance that she would be recognized for she knew that who she was about to meet had a notoriety about her. She entered the church proper and knelt down in a pew near the rear of the church. She then waited for a handful of worshippers to leave the church until there remained one last person. That last person was sitting in the very front pew and had not turned around once. Mary approached the front pew without hesitation from the left side since it was closer to the woman. She was very careful not to expose her face by walking sideways into the pew just in case the woman she was approaching was not the woman she was seeking out. She walked further until she was around four feet from the woman and then she knelt down. Before she could speak the woman asked, "Is it Mary?"

Mary answered, "It is I. Is this Madam Torquet?"

"It is. Is there anyone still left in the church?"

"No, everyone else appears to have gone," Mary answered.

"There is a side room on the left side of the vestibule as you are going out. We can go there and safely talk. I will meet you there in a few minutes," instructed Madam Torquet.

Mary found the room. It had a door with a latch on the inside and a stained glass panel on the door through which some light could filter through. Madam Torquet soon entered through the door and then latched the door so no one could disturb them and then said, "We must speak softly."

"What can I do for you, Mary? Madam Torquet asked in a confident businesslike manner. "You mentioned some type of lucrative offer in your letter."

Mary answered just as confidently, "Yes I did."

"Let's dispense with the names for I believe it will be safer in case someone were to hear us."

Mary went on to say, "As you are aware from my letters to you I am aware of what you are involved in and applaud you for it," hoping that her approval of her trade would lead to an acceptance of what she was about to propose. "I would like to propose a deal that should be mutually beneficial."

Abigail Torquet encouraged Mary to proceed. "From what I know of your business you seem to have been dealing for the most part with clients who are in the lower echelon of society and what you are receiving for your services, I would suspect, are paltry in comparison to what I have to offer."

"What are you saying?" asked Abigail. Do you have someone special that needs my services and is willing to pay a handsome sum? Perhaps it is yourself?"

"No, certainly not myself, and no one in particular at this very time."

"Please do not be wasting my time," said Abigail rather indignantly.

"I guarantee you that I am not wasting your time. How would you like to have a potential stream of high–paying customers, customers who would not want others to know what they have done or what you have done for them?" Mary said.

"What exactly are you trying to say?"

"Can't you see? There is more to be made than by just practicing your trade. These customers have potentially everything to lose and will not want other people to know that they were responsible for the need of your services. They will be most commonly of high status and with significant wealth and willing to protect their reputations, and they will also not want to risk prosecution for involvement with . . ." and Mary said in an even more hushed whisper ". . . abortion."

"What makes you think that I want to enter into this arrangement?" asked Abigail. "And why do you think that I need you to get me these clients?"

"I know that you like the finer things in life. You live on Fifth Avenue. It must take a pretty penny to keep that up! And why do you need me? I have my sources and I am connected with wealth. Men and women of means know that they can trust me because I am not ashamed to help them out with their 'situations'."

"And how then do you plan to blackmail them if they trust you?" asked Abigail. "They certainly will not trust you again. Your reputation for whatever it is currently worth will be gone," she added matter–of–factly.

"That is where you are wrong." She hesitated due to a shadow interrupting the light coming through the stained glass and some noise outside the door. She waited for the noise to end and the light to shine through again before proceeding. Mary continued, "I have taken great care to not be identified with the extortion."

Mary and her husband had already set up a separate bank account at his bank in an account registered to a bogus meat processing and distributor company. The signatories were themselves under bogus names, but the registered owners of the company were not.

Abigail said with agitation, "So you mean to have me carry out this blackmail and leave me dealing with the repercussions if it becomes unveiled?"

"Believe me you will be handsomely rewarded. Four times what you currently receive will be your compensation and that is just for the medical service you provide. And I guarantee that this price will be paid. I will expect ten percent on the procedures you perform on my referrals and thirty percent of the monies that you obtain by means of the blackmail."

"You know the press and the advertisements. What makes you think that these women will come to me?" Abigail persisted.

"Because I will have extolled your name above others regarding your expertise, but you first must accept my deal," Mary said resolutely.

Abigail Torquet pondered for several minutes and then agreed to the proposal. They had also agreed that the women that would come would come with money in–hand. She would then send by courier, through the mail service that they had used previously for their correspondence, the agreed ten percent back to Mary on a monthly basis. The extortion money would be sent quarterly.

Abigail Torquet unlatched the door and left the church. In order to be certain that she was not identified with Mrs. Kent she walked away from any observers so as not to be identified and progressed several blocks before reaching her carriage and departing.

Mary waited an additional ten minutes and then left the church. As she was leaving she passed an alcove which drew her attention. There she saw two paintings, one on the right depicting the Virgin Mary holding her infant son, Jesus, and the other, opposite the first, with the Virgin Mary shown crushing the head of a serpent. Her eyes glimpsed the paintings and she quickly averted her eyes as she was determined to carry out her plan. She rushed out of the church and back to her carriage and awaiting driver.

Chapter Ten

Ginny looked over Collin's class schedule and compared it to her own. She couldn't find a time when they would be near each other for any length of time since most of his classes were in the opposite wing of the building than where she was. The last time they met in the stairway she had been in a hurry because she had to go a good distance to get to the next class whereas Collin did not.

Ginny sent another email to Collin. She said, *Collin, It doesn't seem like there is any good time to meet during the day at school. Your schedule puts you on one side of the building and me at the other. I know we saw each other that one time this year but I had to rush to the other side of the building to get to class in time. So, even if we did see each other, I wouldn't be able to stop and talk. What time do you get done with football practice during the week? If you're done about the same time as I am with cheerleading practice, we might be able to meet after.*

I usually get done and out of the locker room by about ten minutes after six, Collin wrote back.

Boy, you guys stay a long time! I get picked up from practice at five. ☹

Do you stay for the varsity game on Saturdays? If you do, how about you wait for me to come out of the locker room? If we win, I should be out in about 20 minutes. If we lose, it may be 40 minutes.

That should be fine. I'll just use a friend's phone to call my mom to pick me up. I'll have to let her know what I am doing since I usually need to come straight home from the game. But, it should be alright.

Ginny was finally able to settle down and get her homework done. She still needed help from Brian, but it seemed to go much smoother than usual. *Maybe my concentration is getting better!* she thought.

Ginny's mother was still up and reading a magazine. Her dad was watching a late football game on television. Rose saw Ginny and said, "Look what's in this magazine. It is an article about fall school dances like Homecoming and some of the dress styles that girls will be wearing. Here," as she handed Ginny the magazine.

"I was just thinking about what I was going to wear! I really like this one," pointing to one of the pictures. The fabric looks real shimmery and I really like the shade of green." Then Ginny switched gears and said, "Mom, can I stay after the varsity football game this Saturday to talk to Collin? We don't ever see each other during school and I don't have a cell phone to talk to him."

"Poor, poor Ginny," Rose said. "Seriously, I think that would be okay, but . . ."

"But what, mom?"

"But I think it would be best if your friends were around somewhere. I know that you gave me that good report on Collin but I would feel better since you haven't really spent any time with him, or have you?"

"No, I haven't, and yes, Jenny will be around. I'm not planning to do anything if that is what you are concerned about."

"Of course I'm concerned. I'm your mother. You just call me when you are ready to come home. But, don't make it too late. You know that I have to go to work."

"If it is past five o'clock I'll just call dad, but I really don't think I will be that late."

"Okay," said Rose. "By the way, could you have your brothers bring their laundry down? You too, and each one of you separate all of it so I can get some started tonight. If they tell you no, tell them I said they're grounded." Rose then yelled, "Thanks," as Ginny was heading up the stairs.

Ginny told the boys what their mother said and Marty just ignored her. Ginny walked into Marty's room, nudged his shoulder, and said, "Marty, did you hear what I said?" He answered, "What?" He was busy playing a new computer game and really wasn't paying attention. Brian heard her and answered, "I'll get it in a minute." He was researching the campuses of Stanford and Yale. Ginny took her laundry down and separated it, and then went back to her mom and said, "Thanks, mom, for all your understanding and all your help. I really appreciate it." Rose walked over to Ginny, hugged her, and said, "I love you honey."

Before Ginny hit the sack she checked her email one more time. Jen had sent a message about her chemistry lab partner and it said, *We must have some kind of chemistry going on because he asked me to Homecoming. I said yes!* Ginny, ignoring Jenny's humor, wrote Jen back telling her how happy she was for her.

***

The next morning at their lockers Ginny asked Jenny, "Do you want to go to Homecoming together?"

"What do you mean, like lesbo? I thought I told you I had a date."

"No, silly, double date," retorted Ginny.

"I guess that would be fine. Are you sure it's okay with Collin? You know that he's not going to want to go with two more sophomores. He'll probably want to go with one of his buds."

Ginny answered, "You may be right, but I'll ask him this Saturday. I'm going to meet him after his game, and we're going to talk."

"Talk? Yeah, I bet!"

"No, really . . . and have you been talking to my mother? Never mind. That was the only time we could find to meet and talk. Can you stick around after the game? My mom wants a friend to be around just in case."

"In case what?" And then in a whisper, "In case he rapes you?"

"Will you stop?" Ginny appealed. "Why would you say something like that to me? You are the one that said that he had never been in trouble!" Ginny agitatedly whispered back.

"Okay, I'll stop playing, I mean, kidding with you." And then with a grin on her face she whispered, "I'll stick around for your safety after the game. I'll come equipped with my 357 Magnum."

***

The week proceeded better than expected for Ginny. She had received an 'A' on a biology test and on the test paper was written 'Good Improvement'. She also got her second 'B' in a row on a math quiz. She also learned that she was invited to practice with the varsity cheerleading squad since they were short due to an injury to one of their team members. It was important that they had enough team members to pull off one of the cheers and they felt that she had the strength and athletic ability to pull it off. So, today she was going to meet with their squad, instead of her own, for practice. Ginny thought that this was great since they tended to practice near where the varsity football team practiced. She might get a chance to see Collin in action. He might also see her and be impressed that she had been invited up to the varsity cheerleading squad.

After school Ginny went about her normal routine of getting ready for cheerleading practice. She could tell that a couple of her sophomore teammates were a bit jealous but most congratulated her for being invited to help out the varsity squad. Comments such as 'show them what you can do', and 'you go girl' were made to her as she left the locker room.

Ginny found out that she was needed for a series of tumbling moves that required a specific number of girls. She also found out that they wanted her for the pinnacle of a pyramid that they had been practicing. She was relieved to find out that the girl she was replacing had not injured herself from falling from the top but had strained an arm muscle from being near the bottom, giving support. Ginny was nimble and flexible, and she was also the lightest, so she would be perfect at the top.

She would occasionally catch a glimpse of Collin as he was practicing for the next day's game. The football team seemed to be running a series of passing plays requiring a lot of precision. She thought, *He and I have to do much the same thing. We both require precision and timing.*

Soon it was time to practice getting into the pyramid. They practiced until they felt like they were smooth and stable and could do it in a short amount of time. It took them about one hour to meet the coach's expectation and once they got it right the coach asked them to stay in position so that a picture could be taken. They had to hold their positions for what seemed to be forever in order to get the picture, and they were proud they were able to hold still for that length of time.

The varsity football coach glimpsed the pyramid. He had been starting to get frustrated with his charges and stopped them and said, "You see those cheerleaders over there? We are going to practice these plays until your precision matches the precision of those cheerleaders. Now, get back to work!"

Nick, who played left offensive tackle and was protecting Collin as an offensive lineman, turned slightly and said to Collin, "Hey isn't that the girl that you plan on taking to Homecoming on the top of that pyramid? I didn't know that she was part of the varsity cheerleading squad." Just then the football was snapped and Collin was tackled almost immediately.

"Nick, what the devil are you doing? You missed your blocking assignment! Give me five laps, now!" yelled the offensive line coach.

When Nick got back, Collin said, "What was that? You know coach doesn't have any tolerance for not paying attention, plus that was quite a hit I took because of you!"

"I was just asking if you'd noticed that your date was at the top of the pyramid. I'm sorry for someone hurting your fragile body," Nick replied sarcastically.

"What do you mean? She's not on the varsity squad. That must've been the sophomore girls if that was her." Collin stated emphatically.

"I don't think so? That is the only girl that looks different among all those hotties today. And I guarantee you I know. I've been trying to decide which of those girls I'm going to ask to Homecoming this year, so I guarantee you I've been looking," Nick answered as if he would certainly be successful in his pursuit.

"So it is purely a beauty contest for you, huh Nick?

"Don't be so smug, C. D. Didn't you say that your date was cute and had a nice smile? Don't tell me you don't look for beauty!"

"Yeah, you're right, but I care for more than what she looks like! How many of those girls do you know, Nick?"

"Oh, I know most of those girls, several in the biblical sense, if you know what I mean."

Collin was not certain exactly what Nick meant by that but had a suspicion. He waited until after they were done with practice and getting ready to leave when he said to Nick, "Were you trying to tell me that you have 'done it' with several of the cheerleaders?"

"What else would I've been saying?" Nick answered in a macho intonation.

"I mean . . . intercourse?" Collin again asked embarrassingly.

"Yes, I already told you that. You mean you have never done it?"

"No, not really. I haven't really been that interested in girls until this year, or actually last year when I met Ginny. But, even then, I was more concerned about studying and improving my athletic skills than that sort of stuff. Even now, I really do not want to get that involved. I have my future to protect," Collin answered Nick.

"Future to protect? What are you protecting? Everybody does it! Obviously some more than others," Nick said beaming and then went on to say, "What are you worried about anyway? There's protection and all the girls are on some sort of birth control."

"What about infections?" protested Collin.

"Oh, c'mon, all those girls are healthy. Do they look sick to you? Besides if you do get something, all you have to do is get an antibiotic from a health clinic."

"And how do your parents not find out about that? Have you done that?" Collin asked the second question before Nick could answer the first.

"As I told you, those girls are all healthy!" Nick answered, ignoring Collin's questions.

On Saturday Ginny cheered at the sophomore game and then joined the varsity squad in cheering for the big game. Neither of Ginny's parents were at the game because they both had to work. Ginny knew that it was going to be virtually impossible for her mother to pick her up after she got done talking to Collin since her mom would be at the beauty shop until just before she was going to have to leave for work at the restaurant. She thought, *on the ride home with dad I can let him know how I did on my math quiz and biology test. That should ease the ride home.* Then she thought, *what am I so concerned about? I have improved my grades. Maybe that strange feeling in the pit of my stomach will be gone now that I am doing better in school.* Ginny, most of the time, had carried an uneasiness in the pit of her stomach when she had to spend time alone with her dad due to his academic expectations of her.

***

The pyramid went off flawlessly but the varsity football team lost by a last–minute field goal from the twenty-five yard line by the other team. And it was one of those that just made it, squeaking by just inside the right goal post. She did not know how Collin was going to feel after losing and she even wondered if he was even going to remember that they were going to meet if the coach ended up being hard on the team. She waited and it was pretty much exactly what Collin had said it would be if they lost. She waited forty–five minutes for him to come out of the stadium locker room.

Collin was looking pretty dejected as he walked toward the stadium gate with Nick. Getting to the gate he stopped and said to Nick, "I almost forgot. I'm supposed to meet Ginny!" He turned around to look for her. He found that she was waiting outside the locker room doors near the track. He walked to her and immediately apologized for almost forgetting about her. Ginny told him that she understood and was wondering if he'd might forget with the loss and all. She asked him, "Was he pretty hard on you guys?" Before answering he quickly turned to see if Nick was waiting for him but found that he had left.

Turning back, Collin asked, "You mean coach?" knowing pretty well that is whom Ginny was referring to. "We expected that. He reamed us out pretty good for missing some tackles and some blocks. In the end, though, he said that we had played a highly ranked team and that he knew we were in for a good fight. He said that we played hard, and that we would learn from this defeat."

"So why were you so glum coming out of the locker room if he let you know that you were beat by a very good team?"

"Because we lost, and we could have won! But heck, we'll beat them next time!" Collin said as his voice showed signs of a lightening mood. He then said, "Only a couple of weeks away."

"You play them again in two weeks?" Ginny asked surprised.

"No, I mean Homecoming. Sorry to change the subject."

"Oh yeah, I know. And I'm not ready for it. I don't even have a dress."

"I'm sure you'll look great. That reminds me. I had better check my sport coat. I haven't tried it on for a year and I know that I have gotten bigger. Thanks for reminding me."

"You're welcome," Ginny said as she smiled.

"I love your smile." All Ginny could do when Collin said that was smile again. They peered into each other's eyes for some time before Collin broke the silence and said, "If you don't mind I'd like to go with a friend of mine and his date. I have a car, so I'll drive and after the dance we can go out for something to eat. How does that sound?"

Ginny said with some concern, "That sounds okay. Do I know your friend or his date?"

"Probably not my friend, but maybe his date. You may have met her. In fact, you must have met her. She is one of the girls that you cheered with today at the football game. Her name is Ashley Gold. My friend is Fred Burnett."

"I think I remember the name Ashley being mentioned, but the squad is pretty big and I really can't put the name to a face."

"You'll probably remember her when you see her. In fact, if you have a year book from last year you can look her up. You can look up Fred too. I'm really not sure why Ashley said yes to Fred."

"Why do you say that?" asked Ginny.

"Because Fred is all brains. I mean he's a nice guy and all, but Ashley . . . I just wouldn't think she would go for a guy like that. Who knows?" Collin had been wondering why Ashley, who just may have been the most beautiful girl in the junior class, would want to go to the dance with Fred. Fred was not only smart but would have been considered to be on the verge of nerdiness. It just didn't seem like a good fit to Collin. He then told Ginny that he thought Ashley had asked Fred to go to the dance and not the other way around.

"Okay, I think going with them should be fine," Ginny responded with doubt in her voice.

"You don't sound too sure about this. What's wrong?"

"It's just that I was hoping that my friend Jenny could come with her date, too."

"I don't really think that is going to be possible with my car. Maybe your friend and her date can meet us after the dance. Do you have a curfew?"

Ginny was glad that he asked her that question. She didn't know the answer but at least he asked, and it sounded like he would respect the answer once she knew what her parents said about it. She wasn't happy that there wouldn't be enough room in his car for Jenny and her date but didn't say anything about that. She said in response to his question, "I don't know but I'm pretty sure my parents will have a time that they'll want me home. I'll email you an answer when I find out."

"Oh, no phone yet?" Collin said, giving her a hard time. "Email it is."

Jenny had been waiting by the school building. She could barely see Collin and Ginny from where she was at, but could tell that she was okay. She wasn't expecting anything to really happen anyway, but maybe a kiss would have been exciting.

"That was boring," Jenny said to Ginny.

"Maybe to you it was," Ginny replied. "It looks like we're going to the dance with a buddy of his and his date. But, he said he didn't think that his car would be able to fit six of us and asked if you and . . .by the way, what's your date's name?"

"Tom Kincaid."

"Maybe you and Tom could meet us after the dance for something to eat."

"My parents already insisted that they're going to drive us to the dance and pick us up. Dinner is going to be at our house, pizza, after the dance," Jenny confessed rather sheepishly. "I can ask them if they'll drive us to meet you for dinner instead!" she added with some excitement and hope. "Where are you going for food?"

"We didn't talk about that. Collin just said that we'd go out after the dance."

"I'll talk to you later, Gin. There's my ride. Do you need a ride home?"

"Yes, and can I use your phone to call my dad to let him know that he doesn't have to pick me up?

"Sure, and is there anything else I can do for you today?" Jenny asked in a sarcastic tone, but was actually just joking, since that was the second favor she had done for Ginny in the past hour.

Since Ginny had planned to tell her dad about her grades on the ride home, and that opportunity was now gone, she decided to let him know when she got home. When she got there he was happy he didn't have to pick her up. He said to her, "I didn't ask you, but how did your day with the varsity cheerleading squad go? I heard that you were the only sophomore picked to join them. Is that right?"

Ginny was delighted that her dad was talkative and interested in her day. In response she said, "Yes, I was the only one asked, and everything went according to plan. We executed the cheers well, and the pyramid, with me on top, went flawlessly. Unfortunately the football team lost the game, but Collin said they will beat the Falcons the next time they play them."

"I understand that you stayed late to talk to Collin. What'd you talk about?"

"Mostly what we were going to do for Homecoming. He is going to pick me up for the dance. We're going with another couple, and after the dance we're probably going out for something to eat."

Her father then asked, in a serious tone, "So, your date has his driver's license. Is he a safe driver and do you know if he drinks? You know some of the jocks in my day had a reputation for doing that sort of thing."

Ginny was irritated by her father's question and she said, "Dad, are you serious? Didn't mom tell you that even before I told Collin that I could go with him, she made me find out if he had ever been in trouble? He's a very good student, the starting quarterback, and has only had a parking ticket. Does it sound like he would put me at risk?"

Sternly her father answered, "No it does not, but you never know what boys will do and it is not unusual at this age to start drinking, especially guys that think they are hot stuff, being starters on the football team and all. I would like to meet him before the dance."

Ginny, being careful to not irritate her father, said, "He'll be here to pick me up when we go to the dance. Is that fine?"

"No, I would like to meet him before then. How about next week after the football game? Are you going to cheer for the varsity?

Seeing that she wasn't going to win, she answered, "I think I'll be cheering for them, but I won't find out until sometime this week."

"Regardless if you do or not, I'll be at the game since I'm off," Alex said.

"It's an away game next week and the team is taking a bus," Ginny informed her dad, to his chagrin.

Alex was disappointed but said, "Then after practice one day this week have him stop by the house and introduce him to me."

"Are you serious dad?"

"Sure I'm serious. I think I need to see the first boy to take my daughter on a date and to ask some questions. Call him and see if he can come by tomorrow. That would be fine, too." He then said to Ginny, as if they had just had a conversation about the weather, "Do you want to order a pizza tonight for dinner? Brian won't be home but Marty is, and he would like sausage and green pepper. Is that alright with you?"

Ginny had been deep in thought when her dad asked about the pizza. She'd been thinking, *this can't be too bad. What could go wrong? Collin is a nice guy, and he hasn't been in trouble as far as I know.* And then she thought, *I didn't tell dad about my grades.*

"Did you hear me," her dad said, bringing Ginny back into the moment.

"What?" she said, startled.

"Pizza tonight, and is sausage and green pepper okay?"

"Oh, oh sure. Dad, I wanted to tell you something else." Alex turned to her again and waited for what she had to say.

"I got an 'A' on my biology test and a 'B' on a math quiz last week."

Alex said, "Great! Keep up the good work! Do you think that your work with Brian is paying off?"

"I do, dad, and I also think that being on the cheerleading team has helped too. I'm not sure exactly why, but I'm having fun and I seem to be concentrating better. Anyway, I'm going up to take a shower."

"Okay," said her dad, "I will call you when the pizza gets here."

Ginny's dad was sorely hoping that his insistence on doing well in school had finally made an impression on Ginny, and it seemed now like it was. He didn't really care how she was doing it, whether it was Brian's help, cheerleading, or whatever. He just wanted her to do well. Alex was also insistent on not putting his daughter into any unnecessary danger, therefore his desire to talk to her Homecoming date. Not only was he concerned about safe driving, but he wanted to send a message to Collin that he had no tolerance for any sexual shenanigans with Ginny.

As it so happened, Ginny did send an email to Collin on Saturday night explaining to him that her father wanted to meet him either the next day, Sunday, or during the week sometime after he got done with practice. But Collin had been hanging out with some of his football buddies on Saturday night and didn't see the message. He and his friends were commiserating over their loss to the Falcons earlier in the day. A couple of the guys had brought a case of beer. They popped open the cans and started to hand them around. Collin, who had never drank alcohol before, was reluctant to accept, but since he saw that everyone else was drinking he didn't want to look different and went ahead and took a can. He didn't really like the bitter taste so he sipped it. His buddies were already downing their second cans before he was half–way through his first. He wondered why they liked the stuff but felt too self–conscious to ask. By this time his friends were starting to get louder. They began telling each other raunchy jokes, laughing and appeared to be having a great time. Collin just took it all in as he continued to sip his beer. Then Nick said to Tony, "You know, if you would have made that tackle at the fifty you could have prevented them from kicking the winning field goal." That touched a nerve.

"Yeah, and if you would have made the block when we were on their forty we could have gotten a first down to keep our last drive alive!" Nick, who tended to have a fiery spirit on the football field, showed even more of that now and picked a fight with Tony.

"Who are you trying to blame for losing the game?" Nick said, and he took a swing at Tony. It took Collin and the other two guys to keep them from destroying each other. One came away with a bloody nose and the other with bruised ribs.

Tony screamed, "I think you broke my fuckin' nose you faggot." With that Nick tried to get up. But Collin and the other two guys knew better than to let Nick up, or he just may have tried to kill Tony for that comment. After they had settled Nick down, Collin said to him, "Okay Nick, I am taking you home. Let's go." Once in the car, Collin said to Nick, "What the hell did you start that for? We all could have played better!"

"Well, it was his fault that we lost the game," Nick said with a scowl and stilled slurred speech. As Collin continued to drive, Nick fell asleep in the passenger seat.

Collin was thinking, *I'm sure glad that I didn't enjoy the taste of that beer. God knows what might have happened if we were all wasted. But, what am I going to do with Nick? If I take him home his parents are going to figure out he's been drinking.* So, Collin called home to tell his parents where he was and that he would be home in a couple of hours. He said that he and Nick went out to get some tacos and he would be home by eleven.

The tacos tended to help revive Nick, but Collin knew that if Nick had to talk to his parents they would notice the alcohol still on his breath. Collin next drove to a convenience store and purchased some Altoids. "Here Nick, eat some of these," as he handed Nick the box.

"Why?" Nick questioned.

"Not only does your breath smell like crap from the tacos but you can still smell the beer! I'm taking you home and I don't want your parents asking any questions about what we've been doing."

Nick then said, "Not to worry, my parents are out for the night. They probably won't be back till at least two in the morning."

"Why didn't you tell me that earlier, A–hole?" Collin said loudly and with frustration.

Nick answered calmly and with a chuckle, "Because you never asked."

***

Collin didn't wake until ten–twenty the next morning. His parents usually went to the eight thirty church service and had allowed Collin to attend the later service at eleven ever since he started his junior year in high school. They generally didn't arrive back home until after Collin was already gone because they went out to breakfast with their friends after the service. Collin hit the shower and shaved what little stubble he had, quickly downed a few cookies and washed them down with some milk. It wasn't until after he arrived back home that he saw Ginny's email message from the day before.

Collin wasn't really surprised by what Ginny said in her email. He would get this over with before he thought about it too much. He emailed her back and told her he would come over now if her dad was at home. Ginny was home and she was instant messaging on her computer when she was alerted to Collin's message. She answered after she checked with her dad to see if it was okay for him to come over. She responded to Collin, *Sure it is okay now. See you soon,* Collin wrote back. It didn't take long for Collin to arrive since he only lived about a mile away. He rang the Chandler's door bell and Mrs. Chandler opened the door. "Hello. May I help you?" she said.

Collin said, "Hi, I'm Collin Smith."

"Alright and . . . Oh, you're the boy that is taking Ginny to the dance!"

"Yes," said Collin.

"Come in. I'll get Ginny."

Alex overheard the conversation and interrupted Rose and Collin saying, "Don't call Ginny just yet. Collin came over so that I could talk with him. Hello Collin, nice to meet you."

Collin was thinking, *He seems nice enough. What am I being set up for?* He said, "Nice to meet you too, Mr. Chandler."

"Let's go outside," said Alex as they walked out through the front door that Collin had just come in through. "So I understand that you play quarterback for the high school team. Is that right?"

"Yes sir," said Collin, as the two of them walked down toward the street.

Alex noticed the car in front of his house and asked Collin, "Is that your car?"

Again Collin said, "Yes sir." Alex walked around the car looking at it very carefully.

"Very good looking car!" Alex stated.

Collin answered and tried to say, "Thanks, it's a . . .", but Alex abruptly interrupted him, "I know what it is son! It is a 1985 IROC-Z! Let me see the engine."

Collin opened the hood and Alex peered inside. "Looks like an original? Do you know if it's the original or has it been replaced?" he asked Collin.

"It's the way that I bought it. If it's not the original it's the . . .", and they both said simultaneously, "five liter V-8 with TPI and 215 horse."

Alex went on to say, "This engine was a major improvement from the years just before."

"You know this car well then," said Collin.

"Know it well? I owned one. It was my first half–way decent car with some oomph for the years before I got married. I drove this car while Ginny's mother and I dated. Have you had to do much work on her?"

"I've had to replace most of the suspension and engine valves and piston rings."

"You had to lift the engine, huh? You've got the equipment for that?"

"No, but a buddy of mine does. He has an '85 Mustang and we help each other out a lot."

"And I bet that he claims his Mustang is quicker than your 'Z', doesn't he?"

"Yeah, but he won't accept my challenge to go head to head from a dead stop."

"Yeah. They're all talk. They were like that back then too."

"How's the interior?" Alex went on to ask.

Collin opened the doors and said, "I've had to change the carpeting and floor mats. The only real defect is a couple of cigarette burns on the front seats. I haven't been able to afford to replace the upholstery."

Ginny was watching from inside the house and wondering what was going on. "What is dad doing?" she asked her mother, who was also watching what going on outside.

"I think he's liking what he sees," her mother answered.

"How can you tell that?" Ginny asked confused.

"I think that you may find that out very soon." Rose pointed out that they were coming back to the door.

Collin and Alex stopped on the porch before coming back into the house. Ginny and Rose could hear voices but couldn't make out the words.

"It sounds like you have a good head on your shoulders," stated Alex. "I do want you to know that I am expecting Ginny to do well in school and move on to college. I don't want anything to get in the way of her doing that. Do you know what I am talking about?"

Collin answered, "I think I do, but to be absolutely clear, why don't you tell me?"

"Now listen. She does not need to be caught up in any alcohol or drugs or sex. Do you understand?"

"Yes sir, I do understand. I also don't wish to put roadblocks in the way of my future success and I wouldn't want that for Ginny either."

Alex was thinking to himself, *how did Ginny happen to hit the jackpot? He had better be sincere!*

Alex opened the door and they came back in. Ginny and Rose had quickly sat down in the living room and pretended to be chatting to each other when they heard the door knob turn.

Ginny greeted Collin after he entered. He turned to see her and they smiled at each other. While looking at her he was thinking, *I sure hope that by no sex her dad was not referring to kissing because every time I see her I want to!*

Rose asked Alex, "What were you both doing out there for so long?"

Alex answered, "You should see what this boy is driving." Rose looked out the window. "Is that your Camaro out in the street, Collin?"

Collin answered, "Yes, and I understand that when Mr. Chandler first started to go out with you he had one. In fact Mr. Chandler said that it was the exact same year and model." Ginny became wide-eyed and a warmth flooded her as she thought, *this is really freaky but makes me feel good at the same time.* She even wondered if it might even portend future events for Collin and herself. *Could this be history repeating itself? Maybe this is the start of a long relationship.*

Rose then said, "We had some great times with that car, didn't we honey?"

"We certainly did. Rose, why don't you get those picture albums from back then? We haven't looked at those pictures in a long time." As Rose left to get them, she said to Collin,

"If you don't want to stay we will understand. I know how boring pictures can be when you have no personal attachment to them."

Collin, wondering if this were a test, and also betting that it may please Ginny, decided that he would stay. "No, I think I'd like to stay. They may be cool to see." He was right, Ginny was happy that he decided to stay, and the pictures turned out to be cool to see.

Ginny asked if she could get her dad and Collin something to drink. Her dad at first thought that a beer might be nice, but he thought, *I don't want to send a potential wrong message,* so he said, "I think your mother made some iced tea earlier today. I'll take a glass of that with ice."

Collin said, "That sounds good to me, and then added, with sugar please."

Alex said, "These pictures are a little faded but what the heck." They spent a good two hours looking at picture album after picture album. Rose, in order to prevent from embarrassing Ginny made sure to pull out all the naked baby pictures of her and the boys. There were many pictures of the 'Z', as Rose and Alex liked to call their car. The major difference between Alex's and Collin's cars was only one thing–Alex's car was yellow with black striping and Collin's was all black.

In bed that night Rose said to Alex, "Collin seems like a nice young man. I'm glad he decided to stay to look at the pictures with us. I actually think he did enjoy it!"

"I think so, too," said Alex. "And my concerns are lessened now that I got to meet him and talk to him."

"What concerns did you have?" asked Rose.

"We have never met the boy until now. Were you not a bit concerned of Ginny going out with a jock quarterback?"

"Yes, I was, but I had already heard that he was a good student so he couldn't be a horrible kid."

Alex responded, "Well, I had to make sure! When we started talking I could tell that he was respectful and he wasn't afraid to talk, and that is a good thing. Then, of course, I see his car, and that was great! It brought back a lot of good memories."

"I know, and going through all those old pictures brought back even more great memories," added Rose.

Alex then said with a smirk, "And I know that they won't be able to do too much in that car!"*

Rose giggled and said, "You've got that right."

* The '7' had a central automatic shift lever in the front, and in the back seat there was a central hump where the engine was housed, leaving a seat that was like bucket seats to sit on with a full back panel across. The hump was what Collin was speaking about when he mentioned being cramped with six people in the car. The front was even worse with the shift between the seats.

***

The following Saturday Ginny was still needed to cheer for the varsity squad, the football team bounced back from the week earlier to win their football game, Collin threw for two touchdowns and the team racked up a total of two hundred thirty rushing yards. It was one week until the Homecoming game and then the dance, Ginny was getting excited. After the game Jenny met Ginny and told her that it was okay to meet her and Collin after the dance. "Great," said Ginny. "I'll let Collin know. He was at my house yesterday and we decided that we would just go out for pizza."

Jenny said, "At your house! What did you guys do?"

Ginny answered, "My dad actually wanted him to come over. He wanted to meet him and talk before he took me out."

"Oh my God, seriously? What did he say to him?" Jenny asked wanting to know all the details.

"I don't really know, but my dad seemed to like him. They went outside and talked. I was in the house the whole time, but I know they spent a lot of time looking at Collin's car."

"Didn't you ask Collin what he said?"

"How was I going to ask Collin that? Once he came in the house we were never alone. We ended up drinking iced tea and looking at old pictures."

"Boy, that sounds like it was a lot of fun," Jenny said sarcastically.

"It actually was a lot of fun," Ginny said. "I heard a lot about some things my parents did back then and what my brothers and I used to do."

"Yeah, like what?" Jenny asked.

"Like when Brian and I were like five and three years old, Brian heard that you could catch a bird if you sprinkled salt on its tail. We apparently ran around all day long trying to sprinkle salt from a salt shaker on the tails of birds."

"You guys were gullible!" said Jenny laughing. "No wonder you had fun! I wish I would have been there!"

"It also turns out that my dad had the same kind of car that Collin has when my parents first started dating. So we heard a lot of stories about trips they took in that car."

"Like drive–in movies and . . .? Mm, maybe they wouldn't mention things like that," said Jen.

"Stop that Jen!" Ginny said.

"You don't think they were making–out and who knows what else back then?" Jenny asked Ginny incredulously.

"Okay, enough of this. This not something I want to think about!" pronounced Ginny, and that conversation was over.

***

The next week was all about the upcoming Homecoming at the high school. Each class was busy in preparing their Homecoming float for competition. The winner would be announced at the game. School pride was in display with banners reading, "Go Cowboys" and "Meredith High School–The Best" draped outside the building's entrances. The cheerleaders were busy practicing new cheers, several of them being submitted by students from the school. With that and more, Ginny and Jenny were preparing their wardrobe for the dance. Not only did they need to get the perfect dress, but they also needed the right make–up, shoes, nails and perfume. They were going to have their hair styled by Rose because she was the expert. Rose didn't know this yet, but they knew that she would be excited to do it for them. Ginny also knew that her mom would be disappointed if they didn't ask her to do it.

***

It was now Saturday, a week before Homecoming. Ginny's mom worked only until noon at the salon and had time before she had to go to the restaurant to work that evening. She was not really thinking of anything except relaxing since it was a very busy morning, so she decided to take a nap before going to the football field to watch Ginny cheer and to see part of the varsity game before she headed off to the restaurant.

Rose was disappointed when she got to the game and didn't see Ginny cheering for the senior squad. Ginny hadn't been informed that the girl she was subbing for had been cleared to return to the squad until that morning and therefore wouldn't be needed for the varsity game. Alex had looked forward to attending the game and seeing Ginny perform, but he had been asked by his boss to do some specialized work. Rather than passing up the overtime hours with the extra money, he decided to pass on the game.

Ginny sat with Jenny at the game and with about half of the other sophomore cheerleaders. Rose had been looking around the stands for Ginny but didn't see her. Since she had gotten to the game after it started she had had to sit high up in the bleachers and to one corner. It wasn't the best vantage point to spot her daughter, but when a cheer started that Ginny and her friends knew they stood and started cheering so loudly that Rose's attention was drawn in the direction of the cheering and she saw Ginny. Rose had Jenny's cell phone number on her phone and gave Jen a call betting that Jen was with the group. There was no answer. "Darn," Rose said frustrated. Thinking it may have been a little loud at the first try she tried again. Luckily the noise had quieted and Jenny was able to hear the ringtone.

"Hello," Jen answered, not having seen on the screen who the caller was.

"Hi, Jenny. This is Ginny's mom. I just wanted to say hello. It looks like you girls are having fun."

"Oh, yeah, we are . . . ." Jenny looked around to see if she could spot Rose. "Where are you?"

"Way up at the top in the corner."

Jenny looked up and could see Rose waving at her. "Let me tell Gin that you are on the line. Ginny, your mom is on the phone and she just wanted to say hi. She is up there." Ginny looked up and back and Rose waved at her too. "Ask her if she will do our hair for the dance next week!"

Ginny did just that and of course Rose said, yes. They'd have to do this before she went to work at the restaurant. Ginny said, "Oh darn, the restaurant. I forgot about that. I was hoping that you would be home to see us before we went to the dance." She meant Collin and her.

Rose said, "I'm having a hard time hearing you. You have fun and I'll talk to you tomorrow."

This time the team squeaked out a win by taking a punt return into the end–zone with thirty seconds left in the game.

***

The next day as they were driving to church Ginny said to her parents, "Did you hear that we pulled the game out at the last minute?" Neither Rose nor Alex had a clue that the team was close to losing their second game of the year. Alex, because he was not at the game, and Rose, because when she left, the team was ahead by twelve points. Before they even answered Ginny said, "Iggy Heffner scored with thirty seconds left in the game on a punt return!"

"That must have been exciting to see. Too bad I couldn't stay for the rest of the game," Rose said sounding truly disappointed.

Alex commented, "Iggy. You don't hear that name much. Ignatius Heffner, quite an interesting combination!" as he was thinking of the combination of Ignatius, a religious icon, and the last name of someone with quite a different reputation. "What do you think about that name Marty?"

Marty wasn't paying attention to any of what was being said since he was wrapped up in playing a video game on his handheld device.

"Marty, are you there or did you fall out of the car?" Still Marty did not hear his dad. Ginny nudged him and said, "Dad asked you a question."

Marty asked, "What, dad?"

"It's good that you didn't fall out of the car since that would be hard to explain to the police."

"What are you talking about?" Marty said very confused and went back to playing his game.

Brian had understood the connection that his father had made but made no comment about it since he didn't feel it deserved one, and Ginny had no clue what her dad was referring to. Ginny, whispering, asked Brian to explain, but Alex heard the whispering and said, "Everything said needs to be said so all can hear. You know the rules."

So Ginny said, "I don't have a clue what you are talking about, dad."

Alex said to Brian, "Explain it to her, son."

"Dad thinks it is interesting to have an unusual first name that is commonly associated with a saint in connection with a last name that would not generally be associated with sainthood."

Ginny said, "Huh?" as she said confusedly, "St. Iggy?" and Brian said, "I'll explain it to you later."

After arriving back home Ginny told her mom what she was trying to tell her at the game. "What I was trying to say is that I forgot that you would have to work and wouldn't be around when Collin picked me up for the dance. I wanted you to see us together with my dress and everything. I also wanted your help with my makeup!"

Seeing Ginny's sad–looking eyes, Rose said, "We can do a dry run before I leave and maybe you won't even have to apply the makeup again before you leave for the dance. Just take a look at yourself and apply only what you need."

"But . . ."

"Shush! You'll be fine. And if you want me to see you two, why don't you come to Luciana's for your pizza after the dance. You were planning on pizza, weren't you?"

"The restaurant is a bit fancy for pizza isn't it?" Ginny asked.

"Oh, no. We get a lot of people who just want pizza. And the price isn't more than anywhere else if that is what you're worried about."

"Okay, I'll ask Collin if it's okay with him. Can I call him now?"

"Well, heck yes!" and Rose handed Ginny the phone before Ginny could pick it up herself.

Collin was holding onto his phone when it rang and when he saw it was a call from the Chandler house he answered it saying, "Ginny?"

Ginny, quickly and with barely taking a breath, stated and asked,

"Collin, my mom would like to see us before we leave for the dance but she's going to be at work and she won't get to see us. Do you mind if we have pizza at the restaurant she works at rather than at Rinaldis? She says it's just as good and the price is no different either."

"Whoa, say that again, and maybe a little slower."

Ginny repeated more slowly what she had said and Collin responded, "It's okay with me, but I better ask Fred first. And then, I suppose, he'll have to ask Ashley."

"Can't you just tell Fred that you decided?" asked Ginny, thinking that maybe Fred would just follow Collin's lead.

"No, I may get to call some plays in the huddle but Fred should have a call in this."

Ginny persisted saying, "My mom really would like to see us. Please see if you can get Fred to say yes."

"I promise I'll ask Fred."

"Can you call him now?" asked Ginny.

"I'll try and I'll call you back. Whose phone are you using today?" Collin asked.

Ginny got the hint that Collin was wondering if she had finally gotten her own cell or if she was using someone else's. She said, "It's my mom's. You can call me back at this number."

Even though Collin thought it would be okay with Fred he just wanted to check and not assume that it would be okay. He found out that convincing Fred to go somewhere other than Rinaldis was harder than he thought. Fred kept on saying that no other place had better sauce than Rinaldi's and he had tried them all. When Collin asked him if he ever tried the pizza at Luciana's, Fred had to admit that he had never tried it there. So, when he explained that Ginny's mom worked there, and that she wasn't going to be able to see Ginny before she left for the dance, he agreed to give Luciana's a chance. Collin called Ginny back and told her the good news.

*****

It was now Friday, the day before the big day, and there was even more hoopla. There was a colossal pep rally with cheers, band music and inspirational speeches for the players. This was followed by a parade through the city streets that included cars of any students that could and wanted to drive. Of course they honked their horns and screamed from the windows. A bit obnoxious, yes, but excused and expected by all because it was Homecoming.

Saturday morning was beautiful and the sophomore team trounced the Cougars. It wouldn't be until one o'clock before the varsity game started so Ginny went home to take her shower and do her nails because she knew there wouldn't be much time to get her hair and make–up done before her mother had to leave for work. She got Jenny to do the same. Brian drove the girls back to the varsity game since he was going anyway. He enjoyed watching football but never enjoyed playing it. He had played once and never understood why anyone wanted to be hit and risk injury. He'd been hit and didn't like it. He remembered telling his dad when he had asked him when he was younger why he didn't try out for any of the teams, "Are you kidding me! I got hit hard one time just goofing around and I didn't like it. These guys are risking bodily harm each time they get hit, and if they get hit hard enough that may be all she wrote.

I'm not willing to take that chance. I'll watch, but I'm not putting my health on the line." He was always the analyzer, weighing the positives and the negatives.

The varsity game was low-scoring with both the teams playing magnificent defense. After another pass was knocked out of the air by a defensive back Brian said, "Can't they see that the defensive backs are quick and they are slowing down our receivers from coming off the line? We need to run more and or throw to the backs more." His friend Ralph chimed in with, "We need to try a screen." The team started to run more, making some progress, and with a second–down and one–yard–to–go they crossed up the other team by deciding to flare the tight end underneath the wide receiver. The pass to him was complete and he took it down the sidelines for a long gainer. A draw play gained another eight yards up the middle, and even though stopped from gaining another first down they were able to score a field goal. They were now up by four with less than a minute to play. Brian said they needed to squib the kickoff down the field to keep it away from the other team's star kick–off returner and that is exactly what they did. They stopped them at the thirty – five and picked off a pass on the subsequent third and five, assuring the win.

***

"You girls look so beautiful!" Rose said as they were finishing putting on their make-up. "I wish I could stay to see you leave tonight. Both of you make sure you have fun!"

Jenny said, "Thanks, Mrs. Chandler. You're the greatest. My mom should be here soon to pick me up. I'll see you later tonight at Luciana's." Just as she said that the doorbell rang and it was Jenny's mom.

"Rose, thanks for doing this for Jenny. They both look gorgeous," Jenny's mom said. "C'mon Jen, we need to get moving."

As Rose was going out the door as she left for work she called back into the house, "Alex! Make sure you take some nice pictures before Gin and Collin leave tonight. Please promise me!"

"I've got the camera right here, and I'll take some on my cell too and send them to you tonight."

"You're so sweet. Just as sweet as when we first met. Thanks honey."

A few minutes later Marty arrived home from soccer practice. He took a glance at his sister and said to her, "What is all that junk on your face?" Although he was fully aware of make–up he had never seen his sister wear any, so he took his opportunity to give her a hard time.

"Stop it Marty. Don't you start making jokes! Mom and I spent a lot of time doing this just right."

Marty actually was interested in a girl in his class who was very pretty and when he saw his sister he could not help but think to himself, *she looks great*. Thinking that made him feel creepy, but she did look good.

Ginny was now standing on the bottom portion of the stairs as Brian was about to leave. He came rushing down the stairs and almost bowled over his sister but stopped just in time, grabbing her to prevent her from toppling down the stairs. She looked up at him since she was one stair below him and he looked down at her. He could not take his hands off her arms as he too was so taken with how beautiful she looked. He said to her, "Gee sis, I'm almost afraid to say this but you look gorgeous." Brian then said to himself, *I must make sure that I caution her not to lose her guard. If I think she is hot who knows what affect she will have on her date!*

He started to say to her, "Have a good time but don't let Collin . . . "

Alex stopped Brian and told him that he would handle that.

Before Brian left he asked his dad, "It is okay if I go out with my friends to a movie and pizza, isn't it?"

"It depends," Alex said. "You know what I mean."

"Yes, I know what you mean." And that is all that was needed, for Alex knew that he could trust his son not to go to any movies that he would not approve of. And he knew to be back before curfew.

The dance was to begin at seven and Collin was to be at the house at six–fifty to pick up Ginny. Collin planned it this way so they wouldn't be first at the school for the dance. Since his parents had told him that there was more than a good chance that the girl's parents would want to take pictures he was pretty much guaranteed that they wouldn't be to the school too soon if he arrived at her house at that time. Collin had already picked up Fred and was on his way to pick up Fred's date, Ashley, before going on to Ginny's house. Collin was amazed to see Fred when he picked him up. He was dressed in a white tux with thin black lapels, square black cuff links on his white pressed shirt and a narrow black tie tied to perfection. "You look fantastic, Fred. You posing for *GQ* today?" Collin exclaimed as Fred got into the car.

"If you like this, just wait!" Fred said.

"What do you mean? Wait for what?" Collin asked Fred, but Fred just said, "Just wait and see."

It wasn't long before Collin found out what Fred was talking about. He hadn't gone with Fred to the door of Ashley's house, but when they came out he couldn't believe it. They had obviously arranged for what they wore to complement each other. She looked like a model; dressed in a very sexy little–black dress to go against Fred's white tux. She looked amazing! Collin had a hard time keeping his eyes off of her and could barely speak as she got into the car. She initiated with a sexy and melodic, "Hello Collin, I am glad to finally meet you." All Collin could muster to say was, "Hi Ashley, nice to meet you too," even though he was thinking *damn, she's hot and why on earth did this girl ask Fred to the dance?*

Ginny had just gotten done putting on her dress, her earrings, a necklace and a ring to match that her mother had given her to wear. She slipped on her shoes and was ready to go. She was so excited. She came down the stairs and Alex looked up to see her and thought to himself, *The Lord must have given Rose and me some great genes to share to make a beauty like her.* He said to her, "You really look beautiful, Ginny." Those words made her feel wonderful. She had almost shed all the anxiety that she had held when around her father and this helped to erase the last vestiges. She was almost in tears as she thought to herself, *I'm having such a great time in high school this year.*

Ginny had found a dress similar to what she had seen in that magazine weeks ago with shimmery dark–green material, full below the waist, and ending a few inches above the knee. The sleeves dropped just over her shoulders and the cut of the neckline was from just a bit below one shoulder to the next. Her silky brown hair came down to just below her shoulders and had just enough body that her mother was able to create a wave as it fell over her shoulders and upper back. It was styled back and to the side as to show the beautiful contours of her face. Ginny was not overly buxom but she certainly wasn't flat either. You could say she held her own for being just a sophomore. The fine golden necklace she wore with tiny faceted clear stones and matching earrings just seemed to make her face sparkle.

Ginny was filled with joy and emotion and said something to her dad unexpectedly, "Dad, I love you and mom," and she hugged her father. He was so filled with emotion that he had to fight back the tears that were forming from rolling down his cheeks. He asked himself, *have I been too hard on her?*

Despite his last thought he looked into his daughter's eyes and said, "I know that I have been hard on you but I do love you. You're growing up. It is your first dance with a boy and I am still concerned about you. Please be careful tonight. I know how teenage boys can be. If you believe it or not, I was one once. So don't do anything silly or stupid. You have your life ahead of you and you're still just in high school."

Ginny acknowledged saying, "Dad I know what you are saying. You can trust me."

Ginny went to the window and pulled back the curtain and looked outside. She couldn't wait for Collin to get there. It wasn't long before he pulled up in front of the house. She didn't want to look like she couldn't wait, so she resisted opening the door before he rang the doorbell. In her nervousness she wanted to bite her fingernails, but restrained herself knowing that she had spent a lot of time preparing them. She thought that she would sit down but that felt awkward, so she finally decided to get on the stairs to make it look like she was walking down the stairs when he came in. Collin still had the vision of Ashley on his mind when he rang the Chandler's doorbell. Ginny's father answered the door, allowing Collin to enter as Ginny stepped off the last stair to walk toward him.

Collin's eyes widened as he looked at Ginny coming toward him completely erasing the picture of Ashley that had permeated his mind. She smiled at Collin and his heart started to race. He wanted to tell her how pretty she looked but with her father there he wasn't sure what to say, so he just held out a bouquet of flowers and said, "These are for you".

Ginny asked Collin, "Do we still need to pick up your friends?" and Collin answered, "No, they're waiting in the car."

Ginny's dad said, "Have them come in. I've been appointed to take pictures of all of you."

When Alex saw Ashley he had to keep his mouth from dropping open. She looked much older than she was, and wow! He couldn't believe someone that age could look so mature. He thought Ginny looked beautiful, but this girl filled out her dress in a more womanly way. He wondered what effects beauties like Ashley would have on boys this age and his concern for Ginny welled. He finished with the pictures, taking group and couple shots, all the while maintaining his concern.

As they were leaving he told them to have fun and drive safely and not to take any chances and he then added for good measure, "And don't do anything you're going to regret". Ginny understood. He did not want to be more specific than that and hoped that they all had good heads on their shoulders. But, Ashley bothered him.

Chapter Eleven

"What a wonderful play," stated Jessica Cribbs while waiting during the intermission of *Our American Cousin*. "August Fredericks is simply outstanding in his part. I can see why he got the lead." She was speaking to her group of close friends who all knew August but made sure to include his last name and say it loud enough so that others might hear it also.

"Yes, I am impressed, but not surprised. He is quite a character even when he is not acting!" added Dr. Cribbs. "The gentleman playing Dundreary is quite hilarious. He seems to be getting the most laughter from the crowd, including mine."

"Indeed he is. I was laughing so hard at one point that I started crying! So far, the actor playing Dundreary is the star of the play!" responded John Hughs.

Jessica pointed out by saying, "That is only because he plays the funny character. Everyone is looking for some laughter these days with all the talk of succession and possible civil war. August is doing a splendid job. His character is not as farcical so it seems as though he is not getting as much attention from the crowd."

Beverly Fredericks then said, "August would like us all to meet him in the rear of the theater at the end of the play to celebrate the first night of the production. All the actors and actresses will be there! Will you all stay?"

Everyone was so excited about the chance to mingle with the actors and actresses that they of course told Beverly that they'd be happy to.

After the play Beverly showed them all how to get back to the rear of the theater. Some of the performers who were not heavily costumed were already back into their normal attire. Others were more inclined to just celebrate in costume. Then there were those, both male and female, who had their druthers to enjoy the party while being in the process of disrobing, being partially exposed. The performers had no problem with this but August's guests were a bit flustered by it.

There was food and drink; all sorts of drink. There were the usual coffees and teas, lemonades and ginger pop for the nonalcoholic imbibers, but then there was rum, whiskey, gin, mead, beer and wine to suit the tastes of most of the revelers.

As you may imagine with a thespian group, they were prone to flamboyance, experimentation and inquisitiveness. One of the actors started singing *Aura Lee* and another began to accompany him on a piano and another on the banjo. With that, many joined in song and most others began to dance. As more spirits were consumed, more liberties ensued.

The music continued throughout the evening. Another actor encouraged more to join in dance by playing Bohemian music on his accordion. By the end of the night one could not find a single soul who was not dancing the Polka or the Schottische.

Samuel and Elsa had been enjoying the dancing as well and so had James and Jessica Cribbs. Samuel expressed to James, "You are lighter on your feet than I would have imagined my good man. Did the misses give you your instruction?"

"My bulk in my midsection is no indication for the lightness of my soul nor of my feet," answered James Cribbs.

Jessica quickly added, "It was James that gave me instruction. He cajoled me to start dancing many–many years ago but he thinks I'm some pumpkins now!"

With that James said, "The only reason that you outshine me now is due to your grace."

"We'll, thank you James. He knows how to warm a young girl's heart," Jessica laughed, knowing she was older than the others, as she addressed her comments to Samuel and Elsa.

Elsa commented back, "Anyway you look at it you both look beautiful moving around the floor."

After finishing the dance the musicians took a break and Elsa indicated that she was both hungry and thirsty. The vigorous dancing had robbed her of her energy. As they moved toward the refreshments Samuel smelled something he was familiar with. James, his eyes darting here to there to see if anything was burning, said to Samuel, "I believe I smell the distinct odor of hemp being burned. I hope there is not a fire!"

"Relax, James," answered Samuel. "What you are smelling is indeed hemp, and it is burning, but I believe it is being smoked, hopefully not causing a fire."

James reacted with some surprise since he only knew hemp as a fiber crop, and he knew it to be grown extensively for the strength of its fibers. "Smoking it, pshaw!" James Cribbs said in disbelief.

Samuel, being a pharmacist, had heard of the effects of smoking and ingesting hemp and said to the doctor, "It is supposed to cause euphoria and relaxation and even a feeling like you are out of place with time." They spotted

August and Beverly at the refreshments and commented on the party and how glad they were that August had invited them.

August turned to them slowly and quite deliberately after he had piled food onto a small plate, and with a glaze in his eyes responded, "Aren't we thespians the cat's pajamas . . ." and he trailed off into a conversation on intermingled notes of piano and accordion and how they were the same instrument in a different form.

Samuel said, "I believe he is quite taken by the hemp, Doc! Did you smell his breath? That is what you had been smelling. And I also hear that your appetite gets greatly exaggerated from smoking or ingesting it."

With a raised eyebrow the doctor said, "Ohhh, that's why all the food on his plate!" Doc James then said, "I think that I would prefer the opium myself. It seems you would get similar effects except not the ravenous appetite. And surely I do not need to exaggerate my appetite." He patted on his robust abdomen and said, "If you understand what I am saying!"

August had consumed what was on his plate in two shakes of a lamb's tail. He then invited the doctor and Samuel to join him for a round of oakum smoking. Despite what James said about his weight he could not resist trying this out. He felt it would be good for him to know personally the effects. After all, he was a doctor and needed to know these things. Samuel indicated that he would let Elsa and Jessica know and see if they wanted to join in. Jessica asked Samuel why she would want to do this and what the effects were. When she found out that it could slow reaction time and her husband was going to try it she said, "One of us has to be in control of ourselves tonight and it sounds like that will be me. I will sit this one out."

Elsa was having the time of her life and she was willing to try some new things since she had the chance. She said, "You may be right about someone being in control but what harm can this do? The only thing we need to do tonight is get home and getting into a carriage and directing a horse to get us home does not sound like needing a lot of control."

***

By the time Elsa and Samuel got outside to their carriage about six inches of new snow had fallen. Elsa, still feeling the effects of the hemp, including the desire to eat, commented, "Look at all this new snow. It looks like powdered sugar." She scooped her hand into the snow and started to devour it, laughing at the same time. Samuel started to throw snow at her and before you knew it they were rolling in the snow, laughing, and having one of the best times since they could remember. Their horse neighed as if to show its displeasure for neglecting her for so long for they had been at the party for close to four hours. Elsa, thinking that their horse was perhaps hungry too, said, "I am sorry Winnie, I did not offer you any powdered sugar." She lifted a handful to Winnie but she just snorted and knocked the snow out of her hand.

"That was not very nice," said Elsa to Winnie as Samuel was laughing hysterically from the driver's seat of the carriage.

"Come on now, Elsa, get in. The powdered sugar is coming down harder now," Samuel said, still laughing.

Samuel helped Elsa get in and then he yelled "Trot!" to Winnie, who immediately took off. Not thinking that this was fast enough Samuel clucked, giving the horse license to go faster. Winnie proceeded to a slow canter, but Samuel still didn't like the speed and clucked once again, sending the horse into a faster pace. Elsa and Samuel sounded like school children as they were whooping and hollering. Samuel did not see the next turn but Winnie did! Her turning without properly slowing down threw Samuel off the side of the carriage and then the carriage landed on top of him. Winnie and Elsa also ended up being thrown to the ground but Elsa was thrown into a snowbank and free from the carriage. Elsa, still giddy from the hemp, but otherwise okay, started to panic when she couldn't see Samuel, but she could hear him moaning. It was lucky for her that some of the other guests from the party soon reached where they were. One gentleman quickly came to her aid. He first unhitched Winnie and got her to an upright position. Elsa was becoming hysterical. She could still hear Samuel moaning but still could not see him for he too had been thrown into a snow drift but then the carriage had fallen on top of him. Several other men had come upon the scene and were able to unbury Samuel and made sure he was open to air. They then worked to hoist the carriage off of Samuel. They tried to lift Samuel to his feet but he could not support his weight and readily fell to the ground.

"What's wrong my good man?" asked one of the men.

Trembling from cold and fear Samuel screamed, "I cannot feel my legs!"

Hoping that it was just the cold the same man who had asked what was wrong told his wife, "You go with the Missus here and get her home. Give me your blanket and I will put it on his legs to get them warm and then I will take him home in his buggy since it does not appear to have any damage." He lifted Samuel into the carriage with the help of one of the other men and covered his legs with the blanket.

After they had all gotten to the Ulrich home the gentleman helped Elsa in getting Samuel unclothed and to bed, but he told Elsa, "Keep him warm, but if he has problems tomorrow make sure you get ahold of Doc Cribbs."

Elsa did as she was told. The next morning her husband was still unable to move his legs. Samuel had even wet himself and did not know it. She made him something to eat and said, "I will be back soon. I am going to get James to come and see you."

Elsa had helped him get propped up with his back against the headboard of the bed so that he could eat. He did not feel any pain, just stiffness in his lower back but then nothing below his waist. He tried to move his legs but he could not. He swore, "Damn it all. God, why? Make this malady go away!" He tried to will his paralysis away. He moved his torso to the edge of the bed and tried to force his legs over the edge of the bed but succeeded only in falling to the floor. Unable to move, he sobbed.

It was an hour before Elsa arrived with Dr. Cribbs. Jessica also came in case she could be of some assistance. She thought that perhaps she may be able to help console Elsa if Samuel's problem appeared serious.

Elsa walked into the bedroom and found Samuel lying on the floor. "Samuel what happened?"

Samuel answered, "I attempted to get up by myself, but I could not." Elsa cradled his head to her bosom and they both wept.

James said, "I am going to have to examine you, Samuel. Elsa, you can stay the way you are but I may need to ask you to move a little bit."

"Doc, tell me I am not going to be left in this condition!" demanded Samuel.

James ignored his comment and went about examining him. "Try to move your toes." Nothing happened. "Press the ball of your foot against my hand." Nothing happened. "Try bending your toes upward toward your head. Bend at your knees. Bring your knees to your chest." Samuel could not move anything that James asked him to. Dr. Cribbs also checked to see if he could feel touch or pain in his legs, but Samuel felt nothing. Dr. Cribbs, kneeling, held his head low and said a silent prayer, *Lord, this does not look good for Samuel. If it be your will and power to do so, please help him recover his abilities.*

Dr. Cribbs said to Samuel and Elsa, "As I am sure you already know, it appears that you have a paralysis. It has affected your sense of touch also so that you are not able to feel anything in your legs nor in the pelvic region. With God's grace it is possible that you have only a contusion that has numbed you and your abilities, and with time it will resolve, for I see some bruising in the lower part of your back. I will check back with you in several days. In the meantime, Elsa, you'll need to arrange to have someone . . ."

Jessica broke in and said, "I will help you out. I realize that you need to attend to your students during the day. I will stay and help you, Samuel, while Elsa is gone."

James said to the three of them, "You must also realize that he probably is not going to have control of his bladder function. It is not unusual for the bladder to empty by reflex when it reaches a certain fullness. Samuel, you will need to have to be taken care of in that area to stay dry. Do you all understand?"

A week went by and Dr. Cribbs re-examined Samuel but there was no improvement except that the bruised area on his lower back had turned to a yellow and green color. James returned weekly to check his status but there was no sign of change. Elsa and Jessica had figured out that they could prevent Samuel from urinating on himself by collecting his urine by turning him to his side and positioning a bedpan underneath him. They would do this about every three hours. He could empty his bowels that way too. Doing this prevented most messes, but not all.

A month went by and still no improvement. Samuel said to Dr. Cribbs after his examination, "James, this is not going to get better, is it?"

James answered, "It is not looking so good, Samuel. There is still a chance that you could improve but I believe we have to attempt some other intervention. If we let you just lay here your legs are going to lose any strength that they could potentially still have."

"What are you proposing?"

"We could leave you at home and just passively move your legs, ankles and hips for you, and that may help preserve muscle tone and prevent shortening . . ."

Samuel anxiously interrupted the doc saying, "That is all I can expect, Doc?"

"You have obviously had a very serious injury. The only other thing that could possibly help is a hospital here in New York run by Dr. George Taylor. I believe you are going to need very extensive physical therapy if you have any hope of recovering your ability to walk."

"Do whatever you can, James."

James informed Elsa what he felt needed to be done and set about arranging to have Samuel transferred to the hospital. "You do know that this may take many months and it is also possible that he may be left without use of his legs for the rest of his life?"

Elsa's eyes filled with tears and she said, "I have been losing more and more hope each day. I know we must try this."

Several weeks had gone by since Samuel had gone to the hospital in an attempt to recover the use of his legs and help him maintain his hygiene. Elsa would see him every day. It would take her close to an hour to travel to the hospital after she was done with her teaching for the day. She would spend a couple of hours and then have to travel back home, often not getting there until it was dark. She would often reheat some meat and vegetables that she had made on weekends and have that for dinner. At times she would just pick up a cooked sausage in the city before going home. It was not unusual to have her friends accompany her on her visits, more commonly on the weekends, and it was not unusual for August to visit on his own during the middle of the week. She did not know why he was more inclined to visit than any of the others, but it made her happy. On the days that she would go with others, they would often stop together at a restaurant in the city. On one such occasion Elsa said, "I can see he is being taken care of well, but he does not seem to be making any progress."

Beverly and August were with her on this occasion and Beverly commented, "I can see that the gymnast who is working with Samuel has done an excellent job in preventing his joints from stiffening and has maintained his muscle mass, and that is good. There will come a time when he will soon be standing. I just know it."

August was harboring some guilt over Samuel's circumstance for he felt some responsibility for having invited him to join in the hashish smoking, even though he was not certain that it was the cause of the accident. It was for this reason that he visited frequently. He may have felt better if he had thought that Samuel was improving but he agreed with Elsa that his condition looked bleak. He had admired Elsa's ability in dealing with this hardship in her life for she continued to teach and maintain her resolve to see her husband on a daily basis. He had also still harbored an attraction to Elsa from the first day he met her and he enjoyed those moments during the week when he would still be visiting with Samuel and Elsa would arrive.

The Hughses, Kents, Cribbses, Fredericskses and Elsa still met, but much less often since the accident. When they did, talk would involve the health of Samuel and the hope that he would start to make improvement. Sarah always seemed to be the most encouraging. Her most recent comment had been, "Now that it is spring and he is able to be outside more his mood will improve and you will see progress. You just wait." The Kents did not say too much about Samuel and did not make as many visits to see him, but they did not see much to encourage them that he was making any progress and felt that Sarah was giving Elsa false hope. Generally, after speaking about Samuel they moved onto other topics. They had also continued to occasionally invite Sally Cooke to mediate to the spirit realm. It was during these occasions that Sally attempted to sway further support for causes of interest to her by speaking through spirits. Slavery began to be discussed more frequently during these discussions as it was sensed to be an affront to human decency. Every one of them were all agreed on this issue. Mary had been already drawn into the women's rights movement like Jessica and Elsa but Mary was drawn into it more to help herself rather than to enhance women's self-worth.

Chapter Twelve

Ashley and Fred turned everyone's head at the dance. It was not only their matching attire and Ashley's gorgeous body outfitted with that little black dress but they really lit up the dance floor. No one could hold a candle to them in dancing ability.

Ginny, Ashley and Jenny went to the bathroom together, that is, to talk without the guys and about the guys.

Being without their dates, Collin asked Fred, "Where did you get this star–powered dancing ability?"

"My mom always enjoyed dancing and she taught me and my sister. She said we'd appreciate it one day, and boy, she was right. And Ashley is very good too, but she said that with as good a lead as I am, it isn't difficult."

"Well, you guys are pretty smooth out there."

Nick came by, since his date was in the bathroom with the other girls, and said, "Hey Fred, Fred Astaire that is. You going to give us a chance to dance . . ." and as he was just going to finish saying, *with Ashley,* the girls returned, and he stopped short.

Ashley, while in the bathroom, had met up with a couple of the other junior girls and told them that this date was far more than she could have imagined it to be in terms of fun. They were envious of her because Fred could dance so well. They didn't understand why she had wanted to go to the dance with Fred but maybe this was the reason. They had no clue that the real reason Ashley wanted to go to the dance with Fred was so she could get friendly with him knowing she was going to need help with her advanced math and science courses. She wanted to go to Texas A&M after high school to study and to cheer and knew that she needed to do well in those courses. Who better to befriend than the math and science king of the high school.

Nick actually got his chance to dance with Ashley when a line dance was formed so everyone could have a chance to dance with someone other than their date. It just so happened that Nick was paired with Ashley. Nick did his best *Dirty Dancing* moves and Ashley was up to the challenge, causing the majority of the junior and senior guys to whoop it up. Nick was in heaven. His date was not as happy.

Ginny and Collin had thoroughly enjoyed the dance and had enjoyed each other's company. They were now ready for some food and set out for Luciana's. Ginny couldn't wait for her mother to see them.

In the back bucket seats Ashley said to Fred, "I wouldn't have known you were such a twinkle toes. Where have you been the last two years?"

Fred said, "If you would have asked me out the last two years you would have known sooner."

Being that Fred had been holding Ashley while dancing for most of the night, he reached over to her and touched her hand and told her, "I really enjoyed dancing with you tonight."

Ashley, somewhat surprised because she thought she was going to have to initiate the contact after the dance was over, held on to his hand and turned across the seat sideways and said, "I did too!" Ashley leaned across the separation between the seats and kissed Fred on the lips. That was only the beginning. Silence actually caused Ginny to turn around to see what was going on. Collin could see what was happening in his rear–view mirror and it made him uneasy. It wasn't that he didn't wish this for himself. He was more concerned as to whether it was making Ginny feel uncomfortable. Collin tried to make small – talk and he actually said, "So, what kind of pizza are you thinking of having?"

***

Rose was thrilled seeing the kids come to Luciana's after the dance. Alex had done his part in sending her pictures but she was excited when they came to the restaurant so she could see them herself. She asked the group, "How was the dance."

Collin, who was comfortable with Rose having already met her, answered, "I don't want to speak for everyone else but I had a great time."

Everyone else chimed in with, "Yeah, it was a blast!"

Nick, with his date who still happened to be in a mood, commented while pointing back and forth between Ashley and Fred, "Ken and Barbie here stole the show."

Rose looked at them and said, "You two do look like models for a fashion magazine!"

Ginny went on to say, "Mom, it was more than that. You should've seen them on the dance floor. They were great!"

Rose said, "Oh, like Fred Astaire and Ginger Rogers?" And Nick said, "Exactly! Just what I said," as he shook his head up and down in total agreement.

By the end of dinner, Nick said to Ginny's mom, "This was some fantastic pizza. We'll definitely come here again. Right guys?"

Everyone, including Fred, joined in with, "Yeah, definitely, Mrs. C!"

***

Collin had dropped Ashley off at her house first and Fred walked her to the door. Collin and Ginny should have known that this was going to take some time after what happened in the car on the way to the restaurant. As they continued to watch Fred and Ashley, it looked like they were talking for quite some time and then Ashley and Fred drew their faces to one another and kissed gently. Then it appeared as if Ashley put her arms around Fred to bring herself closer to him. All Ginny and Collin could think of was how good this must feel. Collin wanted to turn to Ginny and do the same right on the spot but hesitated. Fred and Ashley seemed to kiss for a very long time. Ginny then turned to look at Collin. Their faces were now no more than a foot from each other. With the picture of a kiss in their minds they embraced and completed what their minds had started. They were still in embrace when Fred opened the door to get in. He said, "Hey lovers, let me in. You know I need to get home!" They let go of their embrace, Ginny still filled with emotion. She moved forward to let Fred into the back seat and then arranged herself and caught her breath while settling into her seat.

On the way to drop Fred off, Collin wanted to say to Fred, *What were you two doing on her porch for so long, making a baby?*, but refrained, thinking that Ginny might take him the wrong way. Then he thought of saying, *Looks like this*

124

night turned out a whole lot better than you thought!, but he caught himself again before saying it because he thought that Ginny might take that the wrong way, too.

By the time Collin and Ginny got to Ginny's house they had certainly broken a barrier. They both wanted to choose the right words to say, but they also knew that another kiss would come before they parted. Collin expressed how happy he was that Ginny had agreed to go with him to the dance and Ginny expressed how glad she was for him to have asked. Collin then said, "You are beautiful Ginny." Ginny's smile grew and Collin held Ginny and they kissed. Collin then said, "Will you go out with me again?"

Ginny answered, "Definitely, Collin," and they kissed again.

Ginny's father, who had looked out the door and witnessed them in their kiss flashed the porch lights getting their attention. They stopped their kiss and Ginny said, "Darn, I guess that's it tonight. If I don't see you during the week, I'll see you at the game next Saturday." She opened the door and went inside, a smile still on her face.

"By the looks of your smile you must have had a good time," Alex said to Ginny.

"I had a wonderful time, dad," the smile never leaving her face.

"Nothing happened that I would want to ground you for life, I hope?"

"No, dad, nothing happened that would make you mad. I promise."

Alex thought, *she promised and I believe she is telling me the truth. But what's to come? I need to talk to Rose.* He would wait up for her to come home from work, but would wait to discuss Ginny with her until Sunday, after they both got some sleep.

***

Ginny and Marty were home on Sunday afternoon working on their homework. Rose came to Ginny's room and told her that she and her dad were going to take a walk since it was such a nice day and asked her to check in on Marty to make sure he was getting his work done. "You can call me on my cell if you need us. We won't be that far away," she said to Ginny.

"Okay, mom. Could you please let Marty know that you asked me to check up on him? You know if you don't, he'll just say *'who put you in charge?'*"

Rose then went to Marty's room, opened the door and said, "Marty, make sure that you get your work done. I put your sister in charge, and if she comes in to check on you, do not give her a hard time. Got it?" Ginny could hear her mother say this since Marty's room was just next to hers.

"Sure, mom, anything you say," answered Marty.

***

"What did you want to talk about, sweetie?" Rose asked Alex as they walked down the front walk.

"It's probably nothing, but when Ginny and Collin got home they kissed on the front porch . . ."

126

"You're worried about that? I would've wondered what went wrong with the night if they hadn't . . ."

"Would you let me finish? I'm not so worried that they . . . Actually that does bother me a bit. Kissing on the first date? Have times changed so much that it's just routine?" Alex said a bit irritated, and he further said, as the vision of Ashley kept unconsciously creeping back into his mind, "But actually, I was more concerned when she came into the house with this huge smile. It just made me wonder what's to come. You understand where I am going with this, don't you honey?"

"I know where you're going. You're concerned that even though she promised you that she wouldn't do anything that she would regret, she may still do something stupid. That's crossed my mind too," Rose lamented.

"So, you think you should talk to her about birth control?"

"Heavens no!" replied Rose. "How about I just sit down with her and go over where she is with Collin and gradually get into a conversation about the rest of her life and how old she is now and so on? She may not have any desire for that type of activity. You can't say that she wants that from just a smile on her face, and I really don't want to start putting thoughts into her head."

"I don't know what to think. You know that we've tried to teach the kids what we believe but there are so many other influences out there these days. They just don't hear only our opinions. They hear all sorts of crap from television, movies, commercials, magazines, internet, their supposed friends and even teachers. Hell, we even have a guy at work whose daughter, only sixteen, is pregnant from her supposed boyfriend. They *thought that they were in love.* Of course he's not sticking around to help her and how can he, having no job? What kind of love is that? He's only sixteen too!"

"Alright, I see where you're coming from. I don't think we have brought up Ginny to do something so foolish, but I guess you're right that we can't protect her from all outside influences. But, like I said, let me speak to her, and if she gives me any reason to be more concerned, I'll discuss whether she needs to speak to a doctor. Okay?"

"I don't like this whole situation, but at least I feel better with that," Alex said, wishing that this time in Ginny's life, and theirs, did not have to come.

***

Later that evening, after Ginny had gotten done instant messaging Jenny about what happened after they left the restaurant the night before, and found out nothing close happened with Jen, she took a shower and went downstairs to watch some television. She couldn't find anything that interested her. Rose was in the kitchen fixing her lunch to take with her to work the next day when Ginny came in and said, "Mom, I'm bored. I've got all my homework done. I've taken my shower, and there is nothing good on TV."

"Oh, poor, poor girl!"

"Mommm!"

"Okay, sit down and let's talk." And as Ginny was sitting down Rose said, "Tell me everything about your date."

"Well, you got the pictures that dad sent you so you know that Collin gave me a beautiful bouquet of flowers. They're around here somewhere."

"I saw them. You left them on the kitchen table. I put them in the fridge in case you were planning to do something with them."

128

"Like what?"

"I don't know. I thought you may have had a plan to put them in a scrapbook or something. But, go on. Tell me more."

"We had fun dancing and we had even more fun just watching Fred and Ashley dance. But we told you that last night. Collin dances alright, but he could use some practice. I think we both could use some practice. Actually, can you and dad teach me the slow stuff because that is when we had problems? We rocked on the fast songs. Oh, the Queen was Sherri Snow and the King was Iggy Heffner. The punch was mediocre and no one spiked it."

"It sounds like the typical Homecoming," Rose said.

"Then we went to Luciana's, and then home."

"Annnd, did he kiss you?" Rose asked.

"Dad saw us, didn't he?"

"I don't know. I just want to know. You can tell your mom, can't you?"

"Yes, Collin did kiss me and it was wonderful!" Ginny answered as she replayed the moment in her mind.

"I am glad that you enjoyed it dear. You will always remember it. It was your first kiss, right?"

"Mommm!"

"Well, was it?"

"Yes, but why?"

"If it wasn't your first, you may not remember it."

"Oh, I'll remember it. I guarantee you that."

"Well, it sounds like you are pretty fond of Collin. Do you have plans to continue the relationship?"

"We do mom. Why are you so interested? You're the one that told me that teenage relationships don't usually last long."

"I know, but if they last long or not, there may come a time when he may ask you to do something. I think you know what I mean."

"You mean go steady?"

In a gentle manner Rose said, "Well that, but I might as well get right to the point. Your father is concerned, and now I am concerned, that you might go further than just kissing. Now do you get what I am saying? We don't want you to get past first base. That means no fondling and definitely no going all–the–way. And if that is not clear enough, what I am saying is no vaginal, oral or anal intercourse."

"Anal intercourse! Gross!" Ginny said as her body shook as if she got a shiver down her spine. "Are you serious? Who would ever do that? Mom, I think I already told you guys that I knew that you wouldn't want me to do those things, and I don't plan on doing them either."

"I know you did honey, but we just want to make sure that you don't. So, you think that you can stop yourself if you get into . . ."

"Mom, if I can't do second through third base how am I going to skip to the home run?"

"You've got a point. Just please let me know if you start to be tempted to go further than we want you to. Please promise me that."

"Mom, I know I can always talk to you. I'll let you know if that happens."

"Did you get to talk to her?" Alex asked in bed that night.

"We did, and at this point I don't think we have anything to worry about. She respects what we have told her and taught her. She said that if she senses that things are potentially going to heat up with Collin, she'll talk to me. I told her not to go past the kiss stage. I'll ask her every once in a while what's going on. You can ask her too, you know."

"It's just easier for you than it is for me. You know that."

Chapter Thirteen

I must say, since our decision to enter our financial arrangement, business has increased tremendously – increasing by approximately thirty percent. As always, I have included payment for your part as agreed upon. You were also very right in your prediction that some of the clients were going to be willing to protect their good names by agreeing to a premium. They know that I do good work and will not cause the girl they have impregnated to succumb through my means, for if that were to happen, as it very well could, there would certainly be an investigation for which neither they nor I would be able to adequately defend. Your share of these additional collections have also been included for this completes the first quarter of revenues.

As for these letters, if you agree, I will no longer be sending them. I will be sending you your payments as agreed upon, but I feel that any mistake by the courier would be of grave danger to myself and to you.

I trust that you will destroy this correspondence.

There was never any salutation from Abigail Torquet nor any signature with these letters. It was surprising that any letter was sent at all, being that abortion could cause one to be locked up for years. After Mary Kent would receive these letters, she would immediately burn them in her fireplace to dispose of any evidence. Her husband would make the deposits into the bogus account at his bank by himself.

What Mary did not know was that Abigail had started a scheme of her own. She would contrive to borrow money from her well–to–do–clients in order to buy equipment and medications to ply her trade, and then she would delay, or conveniently forget, to pay back any of what she borrowed. She knew that any legal proceedings against her to win back this money would expose her clients to an investigation, and that was something that they certainly would not want.

Mary Kent had taken abortion to be a means of profit on a personal level but she also saw it as a means to free women from the burden of raising unwanted children. She was not alone in this ideology. She also saw it as a solution for women to deal with freedom of sexual expression or as she said *a woman should be able to express her sexual desires as freely as a man does and not be burdened by the occasional disruption of her normal physiology.* What she was really saying was that a woman should be able to play around all that she desires without having to take on the burden of pregnancy. Men could play around freely, even outside of their own marriage, and not wrestle with the consequences of a pregnancy. It was a rights issue, not only to her, but to other women and some men, too. She lamented that laws had become stricter on abortion and she was going to do what she could to try to reverse that. Her means was to continue to sway public sentiment in favor of a woman's right to secure one making sure there were proprietors that could accomplish them safely.

Mary personally did not want children, and Thomas just wanted her to be happy. You know, *Happy Wife, Happy Life!* He was content with material trappings as was Mary. Mary had even had two abortive procedures while they had been married. The Spiritist Movement, which she and her friends had adopted, supported the practice of inter–couple sexual relations as a pleasurable past–time, and abortion became routine if a pregnancy ensued. She was hoping to introduce this activity amongst her friends at the earliest possible chance, but felt that not all would be in favor of this activity. She knew that in order to achieve this she would need Sally's help.

***

Arrangement had been made for Sally Cooke to mediate a séance at the Kent residence two days hence. It was now Thursday. Elsa knew that it would be good to get out with friends. Her days had been long with teaching during the day followed by visiting her husband, who still had shown no signs of recovery. It had been four months since the accident. She was becoming distraught from the ordeal. During her visits to him Samuel initially welcomed Elsa's physical touch and they would often lay together in his bed or sit on a couch and hold each other, but as the days wore on Samuel began to become more detached and depressed, and the cuddling gradually subsided. His caretakers and his therapist continued to work with him to maintain his muscle mass and flexibility, strongly believing that eventually they could strike a change in his condition. So far nothing, but they maintained hope.

The days were getting longer and the weather much more mild. There was still the need of a small fire to take the chill from the house. Everything in the Kent house was exquisite, from the ornate light fixtures to the silk table cloth. Several servants waited on them all and they were offered a beverage chilled with ice if they wished. Most people had been using ice to keep their food from spoiling, but not to cool drinks, so this was quite special.

"You have a fine house, Mr. and Mrs. Kent," stated August Fredericks.

"Mary does a wonderful job instructing the servants on its upkeep, and keeping it supplied with all the newest conveniences," replied Thomas Kent.

"She is talented on the decorating side also," added Dr. Cribbs.

"Here she is," Thomas said referring to his wife, who had just walked into the room.

"You're to be complemented on your home. It is beautifully appointed," James Cribbs went on to say.

Dinner was very formal, with multiple courses, each better than the last. The men again complemented Mary on the delicious food and the amounts of it. The women commented on the dishes, silverware and glassware. "That wouldn't be Waterford, would it, Mary?"

"In fact it would, Sarah. Do you like it?"

"It is very beautiful. I am almost shy of drinking from it, it is so beautifully etched."

"Thank you very much, but don't be afraid to drink from it. It will probably make your drink taste even better than it already is."

In order to prepare for Sally's performance, Thomas made sure that the spirits were going to be able to amaze again. Being that this was his own home he could arrange for a bit more than a window to open. They would be using the dining room table to hold the séance. It was a massive table with its legs being twice the breadth of a man's arm. He had gone to the basement of the house and drilled holes through the floor boards and into the legs through which he threaded some stiff wooden poles. He told a couple of the male servants that he was going to play a little joke on his guests, but they should not laugh or make any sounds during the joke, and not to give the prank away after it was done. He gave them a signal and at the signal they were to jostle the legs of the table so that it seemed to be rocking.

When it was time for Sally Cooke, the usual instructions were given that everyone knew well. Sally then went into her trance. Elsa was not able to concentrate on anything regarding a spirit and ended up just being an observer. Her thoughts were on her husband, and she was actually praying during the period of concentration. Her prayer was interrupted by a moaning emanating from Sally. It sounded as if someone was sick or injured. Then there was a yell orchestrated by Thomas and which was the servants' signal. With that the table that they were sitting at moved upward on one corner and then down again violently, only to have it move at a different corner. This continued for some time and then calmed down. Everyone was holding to each other's hand by this point, some holding on more tightly than others. Then a voice coming from Sally's mouth said, "James, you did not know this before, but you will know it now. This violent shaking and the scream represent what I went through when I was buried alive. I tried to get out of that dark place, but I could not escape. No one came to help me out."

James said, "I truly do not know who this is. I have no recollection of this voice!"

"James, you knew me intimately. You held me in your hands. In fact you held my muscle, my skin, my liver in your hands. Do you not remember?"

Jessica and James were both startled and Jessica said, "You better confess, James. You never told me about another woman. What happened to her?"

It dawned on Doc Cribbs who this was. He addressed the spirit saying, "I do not know your true name, but yes I remember." Jessica was aghast. Her eyes were wide and staring a hole through her husband. "I was thinking of you just this afternoon. I am not sure why, but working in the anatomy lab crossed my mind. I think it had something to do with a diagnosis that I was trying to make on a woman that I saw with a vaginal defect." And then he directed the following comment to everyone in the room, as well as to whom he only knew as Gloria, "I guess you never can predict who you are going to awaken when you think about them."

"Who is this, James?" asked John Hughs.

"Yes, who is this?" sternly demanded Mrs. Cribbs.

"It is the spirit of who we called Gloria, the body that I worked on during medical school," replied James Cribbs.

"You were into necrophilia?" August asked with surprise.

"No, no, just hold on. What is your real name?" James asked the spirit.

"Genevieve Sinclair," answered the spirit.

"Is there anything else that you wanted to say?" James asked inquisitively and with a feeling that there must have been a strong need to have a spirit awaken that was only briefly in his recent consciousness.

"There is. I know in your group here there is a woman named Elsa." Elsa gasped. "I have a message for her, but only for her, for I have been bothered by her plight. Rise, my child, and give ear to what I have to say. Come close to the lips of Sally, and I will whisper through her mouth and into your ear."

Elsa arose and walked over to Sally. The spirit of Genevieve whispered the following, "My dear, you will not be able to ever again have sexual relations with your husband. It is good that the morals of men have been changing as you will reach out for your own benefit to another for your sexual satisfaction and you should not have regret for this. Your friends know that free sexual expression with one other than your spouse is acceptable for the well–being of your spirit living in your extant body. Do not defer your enjoyment any longer."

With that Sally slumped forward, startling Elsa, and then Sally shook her head and awakened from her trance.

Elsa looked bewildered. Did she understand the spirit correctly? Was she being told there is no hope for her husband, and then to allow herself to open herself up to sexual pursuits with another man? She did not want to give up hope in Samuel. She never wanted to do that. What did this spirit know? This simply could not be! But, she admitted that she was craving touch, and with Samuel now losing hope in himself of ever recovering, he had lost interest in caressing and being caressed. Had she not more recently stimulated herself to satisfy her sexual desires? She had come to know that Spiritists often had sexual relations with husbands and wives not their own. Was indeed the spirit of Genevieve saying that this was alright to do? She decided that she would entrust this question first to Jessica to see what she felt about this spirit message.

Before leaving the Kent's residence James Cribbs explained that the spirit, Genevieve, was speaking purely about the entire physical examination of her formaldehyde – laden body and that is why she spoke of their relationship being intimate. Regardless, he was going to be teased about that one for a long time.

After they all left the Kent's residence, Elsa asked Jessica if she could ask her a question. Jessica informed James that she would be with him in a few minutes. Elsa then related what she had been told by the spirit. Jessica was disheartened to hear what the spirit said about Samuel but agreed wholeheartedly that her sexual dimension needed to be satisfied and the Spiritist movement included sexual experimentation and fulfillment. Jessica said, "Do not be afraid to follow what was told to you today. You should not be afraid to express your sexual desires. It is for your own good to do so."

***

August Frederick, in the spring of 1861, was still performing his role as Asa Trenchard in *Our American Cousin,* and the play had maintained tremendous success. It was also at that time the sentiments against slavery had finally caused a rebellion and the Confederacy launched an assault against Union forces at Fort Sumter in the Confederate state of South Carolina. The Confederacy, with a constant shelling of the fort, forced a surrender of the Union forces without a single life being lost on either side, but a bloody and deadly war was about to ensue. Abigail Torquet, meanwhile, was literally and figuratively making a killing with her pregnancy terminations, and consequently, Mary Kent was able to add to her bank account. The increasing revenue was now being generated by a new source which was from women whose husbands were now off to war or were widowed from the war. Many of these women did not need another mouth to feed especially with limited resources. They preferred abortion, but if needed, they would simply suffocate their newborn children after giving birth. And with war and slavery being the issues of most concern there tended to be less effort generated toward prosecuting these crimes, especially if there was no sufficient witness to testify.

For Elsa, her situation was not unlike those women whose husbands were off to war or who had died fighting, except for not having any children already at home to take care of. As time continued to pass, she began to think more and more about what the spirit had said.

August continued to visit Samuel at the hospital, and more often now he coincided his visits with Elsa since he had noticed her sadness and wanted to try to cheer her up. He would often be prepared with jokes to try to lift both Samuel's and Elsa's spirits and he even learned how to do some of the therapies to maintain Samuel's muscular capabilities. He, too, did not want to give up hope for Samuel, and he, unlike Elsa, was not aware of the spirit's prediction that Samuel would not regain use of his legs, bladder and sexual function.

On several occasions August simply picked up Elsa from Philos Seminary where she taught and they would go together to visit Samuel. On these occasions they would stop for dinner in the city. At meal one evening, August reached across the table and took Elsa's hand in his and attempted to look into her eyes. She averted her eyes from his the way she did when they first had met. But she no longer could look for her husband as she did then. Her eyes came back to his and they gazed at one another. He squeezed her hand more firmly. He then said, "I love you and your husband dearly, but I knew from the moment I laid my eyes on you that you were special. I see that specialness in the beauty that I initially saw, and now I've seen that specialness witnessed by your dedication to your husband. I also see that you and Samuel do not share what you once had together, and although I feel compassion for him in his miserable situation, I cannot hide from you my desire for you that I have longed for."

Elsa was being flooded with emotions ranging from guilt to sexual desire. Again she recalled the spirit voice saying to her that it was acceptable, and in fact appropriate, for her to satisfy her desires. Still with some lingering guilt she said to August, "I must return for my horse and carriage but would be more than pleased for you to lay with me in my bed."

Chapter Fourteen

With Fred's help, Ashley was successfully obtaining what she needed to get into Texas A&M. She had recently taken the SAT and scored 1226 and she had also done well in trigonometry and chemistry, receiving 'B's' in each. All she had to do was wait for Texas A&M to let her know if she had made it in. She and Fred continued to date even though she had long ago lost interest in Fred. She had needed to keep up the charade to achieve her goal. She desperately wanted to hook up with Collin, but didn't want to risk it, because she knew it would get back to Fred in some way and ruin, what she felt was her ticket into Texas A&M. When at the university she knew her beauty and her exposure on the sidelines of the football field cheerleading would make it easy to attract someone that might have money – or the potential to earn it–and this would lead her to everything she ever dreamed of.

Ginny, on the other hand, was finding it more difficult to keep up her grades without Brian being around to help her. He had tried to help her long–distance, but without success. She knew mid– term grades would soon be out and was becoming anxious about what her father's reaction would be. With her struggle to maintain her grades she had become easily irritated and rarely smiled. One morning before classes started, Jenny had asked Ginny what was wrong. Ginny had slammed shut her locker and said, "I know that my dad is going to be upset with me! I just can't seem to do as well on my tests and papers since Brian left for Stanford."

Jenny was saddened by what she was seeing in Ginny, and wasn't sure that she could help. She told Ginny that she would try to help her even though she didn't share any classes with Ginny and had all different teachers. "Have you asked Collin if he could help you? I'm sure he'd be more than willing. You know his feelings for you."

"I just don't know how that is going to happen even if he said yes. I mean he would need to spend a whole lot of time with me and I know that he has his own work to get done. I'm not sure it's even fair to him and I might frustrate him. I love him. I don't want to frustrate him. It might turn him off!"

"All you can do is ask him and see what he says," Jenny encouraged.

"But it is more than that! How do I get my parents to allow me to spend that much time with him? I know it's just studying but . . ."

"Give your parents a chance. With the way your dad wants you to get good grades, why would he argue about a good plan to do just that? Ask them and see what they say!" chided Jenny.

***

Rose was preparing sauce for the lasagna she was making for dinner when Ginny came into the kitchen. "That smells great, mom. What are you making?"

"It's the sauce for baked lasagna tonight."

"I want to help, alright? But I've got to talk to you about something," Ginny said and then hesitated.

"What's that?" asked Rose.

Ginny knew that her dad loved her, but still she was fearful of disappointing him, and she answered her mom quite anxiously, "Mid–term grades will be out next week. I know I'm not doing so well, and I'm afraid that dad will get upset with me. And things have been good between us lately. I haven't felt nervous around him like I used to, but now it's all coming back. I sure wish that Brian were still here to help."

"You know that it would be nice if we could have cloned your brother but that's not going to happen. Are you sure that you're not just getting yourself all worked up over nothing?" Rose said as she stirred the sauce.

"I don't think so, mom. Jenny suggested I ask Collin if he could help me. He took most of the classes that I have, and he is pretty smart. The only thing that bothers me is when he would find time to help me."

"Let's hope that the feelings you have about your grades are wrong, but I'll talk to your dad about this plan of yours and let him know what he might expect come grade time. It may ease some anger if you are right."

"Mom, why don't you get worked up about this? You always seem so calm."

"Ginny, we're not all made the same. I think you know that. It's just that your dad had an opportunity to go to college and it didn't work out. You know the story. He just wants you guys to have a chance to not have to work as hard as he believes he and I have to. There is just no way I can convince him otherwise. I know you'll be fine. Try not to stress out so much, but at the same time try to please your dad by doing the very best you can. I'll support you on your plan. Have you asked Collin yet?"

"No, I wanted to make sure it would be okay with you and dad first."

"I'm pretty sure that your dad will be okay with it. You know that he likes Collin, and when I tell him that you are concerned and want to try and make things better, I think he'll go along with it. Go ahead and ask Collin."

Ginny went and got the phone and went to her room. She called Collin.

"Hello?" Collin said answering his phone.

"Hi, Collin. What's up?"

"Not much. How 'bout with you?"

"Collin, I need your help! I'm not doing as well in my classes anymore and I think it is because my brother . . ."

Collin broke in saying, "I'll come over and yell at Marty. I know he can be a real pain sometimes."

"No, no, no. It is not Marty. I think it's because Brian isn't here to help me anymore. You said that you had most of the classes I'm taking now last year and the same teachers. Do you think you can help me?"

"Slow down, Ginny. What is it that you think I can help with?"

Still talking fast, Ginny said, "I was wondering if you could help me understand my subjects better and give me clues on how I can do better on the tests. What kinds of questions did the teachers ask on exams? What were they looking for on assignments?"

"You know I'll do what I can to help you. Why wouldn't I? When do you want to get started?"

"I guess we should have started at the beginning of the year, but too late now. Can you come over tonight?"

"Yeah, I should be done with all that I need to finish by about six. I'll come over around then."

"We'll be having dinner then. You want to come over for dinner? I'm helping my mom make lasagna. I'll just let her know you're coming."

Collin said, "Lasagna? Definitely! I'll ask my mom if it's okay and if it is I won't call back. I'll just see you at your house."

Ginny went back to place the phone on the recharger. Alex was in the living room watching the Cowboys on TV. "Who were you talking to?" her dad asked Ginny.

"Collin. He's coming over for dinner tonight if that is okay with you and mom."

"It's okay with me, but you had better ask your mom, even though she generally makes enough lasagna for an army."

Ginny went to the kitchen and said to her mom, "I think I messed up, mom."

"What do you mean?"

"I already asked Collin to come over and help me, tonight! And I asked him if he wanted to come over for dinner! Is that okay?"

Rose had already started preparing dinner when Ginny asked the question. Somewhat flustered she answered Ginny saying, "It's okay that he comes over for dinner, but I haven't talked to your dad yet! But that might be okay. Collin can start to help you out tonight and I'll tell your dad what you guys are doing. I'm sure it'll be alright." Rose had been crossing her fingers and saying a prayer when she said 'I'm sure it'll be alright' because she wasn't sure it would be alright. Rose then opened a cabinet and pulled out the lasagna noodles and said to Ginny, "You showed up here just in time. We need to start layering the pasta, sauce, and cheese soon. Why don't you start the water for the lasagna noodles? I think your boyfriend is going to be impressed when I tell him you helped make it. What do you think, a little wine tonight with dinner?"

"Mom, you know I have to study."

"That's right. Pop for you two, and wine for me and your pop." Ginny groaned at her mom's attempt at humor. "C'mon, laugh. You must admit that was funny!" cackled Rose as she now sung, "Pop for you two, and wine for me and your pop."

Chapter Fifteen

The football team did make it to the state final and was victorious. There had been quite a few college scouts during the state playoff games, including the final, and it wasn't long before Collin and several of the other players were being called to discuss football scholarships. A couple of the schools Collin saw offers from were relatively close by and included the University of Texas and the University of Oklahoma. He was also being wooed by Florida State. Ginny was happy for Collin but all she could think about was how she was going to survive her final year of high school. First Brian left for college, and now Collin was going to be leaving. She knew that this was going to happen, but now it hit her square between the eyes. And it was going to be even worse with Collin leaving, since not only was he her boyfriend, but her tutor now too. She had learned that it didn't do her any good to start panicking now because there was still another semester to go in the current school year. She thought to herself, *things worked out this year and perhaps I will find a solution for next year too.* And maybe she could learn to study better on her own. Who knew? It had taken awhile, but Collin finally realized that Ginny had to be able to visualize things in order for her to grasp any subject matter, and it was very easy for her if it was hands on, like her cooking. It was certainly a challenge to find how to do that in all subjects, since it was harder in some than in others.

It was also at this time that many of the senior class students were finding out whether they had received acceptances to the schools they applied to, and that included Ashley. The funny thing, and Ginny found this out from Collin, was that Fred was the last to hear the news that Ashley got accepted to Texas A&M. Fred heard it, not from Ashley, but from overhearing her girlfriends talking about it. It was soon after that Fred's calls to Ashley were no longer answered, or if they were, she was always too busy to do anything with him.

***

Christmas break was soon upon Ginny and the semester had drawn to a close. She would not know how semester grades would turn out but knew that she would receive them on-line and in the mail sometime over break. She so wanted to do well in order to return to that good feeling that she had when her grades improved with the help of her brother. She knew at that time that part of the reason she felt good was that her father was pleased with her instead of being angry with her. And even though her mother thought that more involvement at school could improve her grades, she knew that without a helping hand, a tutor, she would have been lost. She had seen improvement again since she had started studying with Collin, and she hoped that she didn't screw it up with a poor performance on her semester exams. It was good for her that she didn't have time to think about this too much since she was wrapped up in cheerleading for the usual Christmas basketball tournament. She was also kept busy by her mom baking Christmas cookies and preparing the menu for the holiday.

Ginny had another incentive to do well on semester grades. She had been told that she would get a cell phone of her choosing if her semester grades were good.

Collin received a text and to his surprise it was Ginny. *Finally got the cell phone. Thank you for helping me get it. :)*

That wasn't the only message that Collin received on his cell. Earlier, he had received a photograph of some girl's breasts in a very revealing bra with the label, *Guess Who*. He didn't tell anyone about it, and he wasn't sure if it accidently was sent to him. He had to admit that it took a while before he decided to cancel the message after he went back several times to look at it. He had seen Ginny in a bathing suit during the previous summer, and unless she had filled out a bit more, he didn't think it could have been her. Plus, he didn't think that she would send a picture like that.

He did text Ginny back, and said, *Happy to help! It's about time! :)*

Collin continued to work with Ginny on her classes when he could. It was a little bit easier for him now since the track season wouldn't be starting for another five weeks thus leaving him only strength work to do. They had been studying, sometimes at her house and sometimes at his. During this time, Collin continued to get more photographs on his phone. The last was of a girl laying prone, wearing lacy black bikini panties. Her legs were bent back at the knees with black high–heeled patent leathers on her feet. There was text added, asking, *do you want some of this? I'm ready, are you?* The girl's face couldn't be seen in the picture. Collin wasn't completely naïve to pictures like this, but he wasn't one to go actively looking for them. But, he was also admittedly aroused by the recent licentiousness. He just wasn't sure why someone was sending them to him. Was it purely a joke? He didn't recognize the cell number and he wasn't about to call to find out who it was. He tried to erase the picture of the girl from his mind but couldn't. Instead he found himself looking forward to the next sext.

As time went on, Collin and Ginny did not always spend all of their time studying when they got together. They'd been going out together for over one year and made plenty of time for kissing. As time went on and the studying became easier for Ginny, more time was spent kissing, and then kissing and caressing. At no time, though, did they remove any of their clothing.

Collin continued to receive the sexts. The last was a full candy shot with the text reading, *Ready to hook-up? I am! Ashley*. As Collin continued to stare at the picture, he got hard. The picture brought back the memory of Ashley filling out that *little black dress* on Homecoming more than a year earlier. He remembered that he could barely take his eyes off of her. He fought off the stimulation he felt as he was about leave to pick up Ginny for a night of study at his house.

When Collin and Ginny arrived back he told his mother that he had to finish a lab report for his physics class and that they, meaning he and Ginny, would be up in his room finishing their homework. His mother said, "Your father had to work late tonight. We're going to the Hyde's to play Bridge tonight so I am going to meet him there. I left some dinner in the fridge that you can heat up if you both get hungry."

Collin got done with his lab report and quizzed Ginny for her upcoming test. He told Ginny that he was going down to get a snack and asked if she wanted anything. She asked for a Coke and told Collin that she had one more thing she needed to study, then she would be done. Collin rummaged around the kitchen and got Ginny's Coke and then found some Goldfish crackers. He went back up and found Ginny finishing up her work. She was sitting on the floor with her back to him. He said to her, "Ginny, turn around." She turned around and looked as he threw her a Goldfish and it bounced off her forehead. "Throw me another." She caught it in her mouth and then said, "Give me some." They continued throwing them one at a time to each other and catching most of them. Collin started to throw them faster and Ginny followed suit, with few now being caught, most winding up all over the room and getting caught in each other's hair. Once the crackers were gone Collin crumpled up the bag and threw it at Ginny and before she could throw it back at him he tackled her. They rolled around the floor until they were out of breath and then lay on their backs. Collin impulsively turned toward Ginny and gazed into her eyes, and they kissed a long and satisfying kiss. Ginny ran her hand through Collin's hair and they kissed again, and again, and again. The picture of Ashley's breasts suddenly flooded Collin's mind. Without hesitation, he took his right hand and stroked Ginny's left breast and Ginny's heart started to beat faster. She put her hand under his shirt and stroked his chest. All Collin could see now was the picture of Ashley's firm buttocks and her exposed genitalia and he was starting to harden. Before they knew it their T-shirts were off and Collin had unloosed the clasp on Ginny's bra. "I love you," Collin said, and Ginny said, "I love you too." They had progressed to removing each other's jeans and had now started to caress each other. Collin said, "Oh-h Ginny," and then, "Are you using any birth control?" and Ginny whispered as her mind was being robbed by her brain's pleasure center, "Don't worry, I just started to bleed. We should be safe." The faces of her parents flashed briefly through Ginny's consciousness but it was too late.

Chapter Sixteen

Elsa had continued to have relations with August. This continued on a regular basis and followed the scenario that occurred on the first occasion. Elsa was somewhat concerned when her regular flow had not come down like it usually did but she thought that perhaps she was getting sick. Or perhaps, it was the stress of the whole ordeal with Samuel and his loss of hope in his situation.

She arrived at the hospital on a very mild and sunny Saturday late in May. She was hoping that she could get Samuel to go outside for a spell because she thought that it might lift his spirits. When she arrived, her husband's nurse rushed out to her. "I've got the most wonderful news," she said to Elsa.

"No . . ." Elsa's eyes started to tear, ". . . is he starting to move?" and the nurse was shaking her head up and down and waving her arms, motioning her to come inside. Elsa rushed to Samuels's side and hugged him. He was smiling from ear to ear, and he was so glad to see Elsa. There were tears of joy in his eyes.

"It was amazing. My therapist was working with me, flexing my legs this way and that, like he always does. He laid down my right leg and then started to work on the left, and he said, "Come on Samuel, give it a try today. Wiggle your toes. And damn it if I didn't move my big toe up towards my head. And if I didn't know better, I thought I could feel Daniel's touch when he lifted that leg."

"Where?" Elsa asked.

"On the top of the foot and the side of my calf!"

Elsa, jubilant, asked the nurse if Samuel's therapist was still there, and he was. "Can you ask him to come talk to me? Or, if he is busy, I will go to him." She wanted to see what he felt about this achievement.

While the nurse had gone to see if Daniel was available Elsa couldn't help but continue touching other places on her husband's legs and feet to see if he could feel anything more.

Daniel excused himself from his current patient and went to see Elsa. "Can I help you Mrs. Ulrich?"

Bubbling with excitement, Elsa answered, "This is so exciting and encouraging, is it not, Daniel?"

"Oh, for sure, Madam. We have maintained his muscle mass and now he is starting to have some feeling and a slight bit of movement. I certainly hope that this is the start of his ability to come back. We will just have to continue to work hard and we'll see."

"Thank you, Daniel. Thank you so much. This is such great news." She returned to Samuel and asked him to wiggle his toe. He did and she hugged and kissed him again.

***

Samuel continued to make strides in recovering from his paralysis. He was now able to feel when he needed to urinate. Unfortunately he still did not have full use of his legs to get himself to use the facilities. At least he was able to alert an aide who was then able to get him there by wheelchair instead of having to use a bedpan. It was now almost the summer solstice and he had recovered most of his sensation, but was still having some difficulty flexing at his hips. Elsa, by this time, still did not have her flow and she was getting nervous. She was finding herself urinating more frequently and feeling unusually nauseous in the morning hours. She did not need anyone to tell her what it was, for she was pretty certain she must be pregnant, pregnant from her encounters with August, even though she had stopped this activity once Samuel started his recovery. She questioned whether she should try to find out if there was something else wrong with her. Perhaps it was a touch of sugar, or maybe some type of infection? She tried ingesting some ginger beer to see if it would settle her stomach, but that did not help, and mint tea had no effect either. She decided to confide in August as to her symptoms and the lateness of her flow. She made sure that she went to the theater shortly after one of his weekend performances so as to not have this revealed in front of his wife, Beverly.

August was just making his way out of the theater and was saying good night to the other actors and actresses that were leaving at the same time as he.

Elsa waited for August to finish his goodbyes and then greeted him. "August, I need to speak with you."

"Hello, Elsa, did you see the show tonight?"

"No, August, I came to see you because I need to talk to you."

"What is it?"

"I believe that I am pregnant and I am not sure what to do. I can't stay this way. I mean I need to do something because it is not Samuel's! You know that he is getting better and he will certainly know that the child is not his. What am I to do?"

"Are you absolutely sure, Elsa? Couldn't something else be wrong?"

"I don't believe so, August. I have tried ginger and mint to try to relieve my stomach upset which has caused me to vomit, and although they work for a time, the nausea returns. I know that this is not unusual early on in pregnancy."

August knew who to go to. "I will take care of this. I will find out who can take care of this for you."

Since Elsa did not go directly to Mary Kent he had figured that she was not aware of Mary's connections. He went directly to the Kent home and found that they were in. He asked the servants if he could talk to the Kents. The Kent's servants recognized August from prior visits and asked him to come in while they went to get Thomas and Mary.

Thomas greeted August saying, "August, how are you. This is a nice surprise, but so late on a Friday evening. What can we do for you?"

"I know a woman who needs your help. She needs to know whom she can go to in order to restore her to her regular cycle."

Mary answered, "August, yes I can tell you who she may go to. She is the best, but tell this friend of yours that she should say that she read an ad in the newspaper if your friend is asked how she became aware of her services. This will protect you." Mary did not want August to be shaken down for extra money like so many wealthy men of New York had been by Madam Torquet, even though Mary would get a handsome profit from this extra money. Mary was not willing to go after her friends and she was not clear as to how much wealth the Frederickses had anyway. Besides, life could become hell if you were implicated as an accessory to the crime of abortion, and therefore, she did not want that for August if he did not pay should Abigail claim he was an instrument for Elsa's abortion. She also did not want to risk the same accusation for herself.

August did not wait until the next day to tell Elsa what she should do but went to her immediately to tell her. He also made certain to include the instructions on what to say if asked where she had learned about Madam Torquet's services. Since it would be Saturday the next day, a day that she did not have to teach, Elsa decided that she would go to Abigail Torquet early the next morning.

She arrived the next morning and was greeted by Abigail herself. Elsa was asked how long it had been since she last had her flow, and Elsa said that she thought it was at least ten weeks. They then went into an interior room where Elsa was instructed to remove her dress and drawers, and to sit down on the table. It was a wooden table with a clean white sheet laid on top of it and a small pillow for her head. She was also instructed to have her fee of one–hundred and fifty dollars ready, and if she did not have it, she would have to come back the next day with money in–hand. Elsa knew that she needed to come prepared since August was informed by Mary Kent that it may cost up to two–hundred and fifty dollars, depending on the largeness of her womb. Elsa had been nervous all morning, but felt that with what she was required to pay, maybe it would not be all that bad. She had not asked what was going to be done to her, but she proceeded to do as she was told. Abigail Torquet had gone to another room to prepare what she needed in order to perform the procedure. In that room she had a wood–burning stove on which were two pots, one which contained water and metal instruments, and the other with a mixture of salt and water. Whereas many women who underwent a surgical end to their pregnancies ended up with complications and even death, Abigail had been able to retain her renown by being able, for the most part, to prevent those things from happening. She was also able to maintain comfort during the whole ordeal.

Abigail Torquet came back into the room and could see that Elsa had done as she was told. Abigail proceeded to take her payment. She then proceeded to give Elsa a glass of rum to drink laced with opium. "I want you to drink this. This will help you to relax and prevent any discomfort. When you are done drinking all of it, I want you to lie down on this table and bring your buttocks down to the edge." Abigail then slid out two additional planks of wood on either side of the foot of the table which had circle cut outs towards their ends. "You will put your heels into these openings to rest your feet. Then you will need to relax your legs so that they will fall outward to the sides. These supports will help to prevent injury to your hips. You will then pull your chemise up to your hips. Once you are relaxed adequately I will place a device into your vaginal opening in order that I may be able to see the entry to your womb. You may feel some pressure as I place it and adjust it in order that I may see well. I will then place smooth metal rods in the opening of your womb so that I can make it large enough to finish the procedure. Abigail could see anguish in Elsa's eyes and said to her, "Do not be afraid! These instruments are not large and they will not harm you. Do you have any questions?"

Elsa's anguish over the instruments was mitigated, but she still anguished over whether she was doing the right thing. She finally asked, "I will be alright, won't I?"

Abigail assured her that this was a routine procedure and that she had nothing to worry about.

Chapter Seventeen

It had been two weeks and Ginny couldn't believe what she had done. *It was an awesome feeling. It was wonderful,* she said to herself. If that is what Nirvana was, she certainly wanted to have more. But, at the same time, she didn't feel good, because she knew that she had let her father and mother down. She had promised not to let it get that far. She asked herself, *should I now ask mom about seeing a doctor so I can get started on birth control?* But, she didn't really know if this would happen again, since she and Collin didn't really talk about it since it happened. She knew it was probably a mistake that they did it. *What should I do?* she asked herself. *Maybe I should tell Jenny and get her opinion,* she thought, as she struggled with herself. *But I don't know what she'll think of me if I tell her.* She didn't think Jenny had done it, even though she often joked about it. *She's my best friend though. I should be able to trust her to tell me what she thinks without her criticizing me. Well, maybe she will criticize, but I have to tell someone, otherwise I'm going to make myself crazy.*

Collin had had pretty much the same thoughts about what they had done. He too felt he had betrayed both his parents and Ginny's. He was also concerned that if Ginny was not right about where she was with her period that they could be in a real mess. He hadn't talked to Ginny about any of this because he was having a hard time sorting things out in his head. But now, he felt he had to talk to her about it.

Collin called Ginny and told her that he had to talk with her, but not on the phone. So they met after school the next day and drove to a park on the other side of town so they would have less chance of running into anyone they knew.

Collin said with confused emotions, "I am sorry, and I'm not sorry, for what happened the other night. I do love you, and it was the most wonderful feeling that I've ever had, even better than winning the state football championship. But, I feel that I have let you, your parents, and my parents down."

Ginny replied, "I feel exactly the same. It was so wonderful that I so much want to do it again, but I don't want to take the chance of getting pregnant at this time in my life. My father would probably want to kill me if I did. Do you think I should get birth control or do you think that we shouldn't do this anymore?"

Collin wasn't sure what to say. He knew that he loved her in an emotional, and now, in a much more physical way, and he couldn't decide whether he wanted that to stop now that it had started. With a sudden revelation he said to Ginny, "If I could have it my way I would want you to start on birth control so that we could continue something that felt so awesome. But, look at where we are in our lives. We're just in high school and there is a good chance that we may not be near each other next year. What happens if our lives grow apart because of that? If I could be sure that we were going to spend our lives together, and if I could support you now if you were to get pregnant, then I would say get the birth control and let's go. But I'm not sure that I want to take a chance that something would happen. Maybe we should put a lid on this and try to find a way to love each other without going all–the–way?"

Relieved, Ginny said, "Collin, I'm glad that you just said that. But, I'm not certain that I can refrain from not wanting to do it again. I was going to ask Jenny her opinion of what I should do, but now I think I know the answer. Let's do our best to stop ourselves from going that far again. I know this is going to be hard, but let's try, because I want to keep you even if you are away from me next year."

Ginny felt better that she didn't have to tell Jenny what she and Collin had done. But, she also was convinced that she may not be able to hold herself back from having it all with Collin again. If he was not strong enough, she knew she would not be able to stop herself. She decided to tell her mom that she felt it was time to see the doctor to discuss birth control, and most likely start it, 'just in case'.

***

Ginny was a bit apprehensive going to see a gynecologist for the first time but her mother said that she would be fine and she didn't think the doctor always had to do a full genital exam on the first visit. None the less, Ginny didn't even feel comfortable talking about her female parts with her mother, or her best friend, let alone someone she had never met before, and that person may even want to look at those parts. But she knew she had to do it.

It was now three–and–a–half weeks since she had had intercourse with Collin, and she thought her period should be coming in about five days based on her normal cycle. She had to answer the questions of how frequent her periods were, how many days it usually lasted and how heavy it was on the intake forms at the doctor's office. These questions started to make her think since the last bleed was lighter and much shorter than her usual ones.

When she was called to be taken into an exam room she learned that she would initially be seen by a nurse practitioner, and she was asked if she wanted to be seen alone or whether she wanted her mother to go in with her. Ginny turned, looked at Rose, and asked, "What do you

160

think?" Rose looked perplexed because she was under the impression that she would be going in with her daughter, but realized that this was something that Ginny needed to decide for herself, and so she said, "Honey, maybe it is best that you discuss this with the nurse yourself. If you need me, I am sure she can call me in. I'll be right outside." The medical assistant acknowledged that that would be a good idea and asked Rose to have a seat in the waiting room. In the exam room Ginny was asked several more questions to expand on what she had filled out on her intake forms. One of those was whether she had been, or was currently, sexually active. Ginny reluctantly answered, "Yes, but only once." She did not want to be perceived as a 'bad girl'.

The nurse then asked, "Can you tell me when that was?"

Ginny replied, "Three–and–a–half weeks ago."

The nurse practitioner followed that answer with, "Based on what you said was your last period, you should be getting your next very soon, in fact, in about five days."

Ginny said, "That's exactly what I figured out." Then the nurse practitioner asked, "Do you feel like you are going to get your period? I mean, are you starting to get any usual symptoms before your period like a bit of breast tenderness or some bloating, weight gain or moodiness?"

Ginny admitted that she felt that her breasts were a little tender but also said that this did not happen routinely before her flow. The nurse then asked her if the boy or man that she had intercourse with was someone she was familiar with and whether she had any concerns that he could have a sexually transmitted disease. Ginny was dumbfounded by this question and did not know how to answer, but she said, "I certainly hope he doesn't have any diseases! Why?" The nurse explained that there was a one in four chance of a sexual infection in active teens and caution was needed to prevent any major harm. She then asked Ginny if they had used any protection against infection and Ginny said, "Like what?" The nurse went on to say, "Like a male or female condom," and Ginny said, as she was starting to get more nervous, "No, we didn't."

The nurse practitioner then said to Ginny, "I know that you came to discuss and start on a birth control method and we will get to that, but I feel that we need to examine you today to make sure that you may not have been exposed to a sexually transmitted disease. I am going to leave you some information on birth control methods and you can start to look at them. I also want you to take off your clothing from the waist down and then have a seat on the exam table. I think it would be good for you to be seen by the doctor instead of me today. I will return with the doctor shortly." With that the nurse practitioner left the room and Ginny became so anxious that she wanted to scream for her mother. *What did I get myself into?* she thought to herself.

It ended up being close to fifteen minutes before the nurse and doctor came to the room.

"Hello, I am Dr. Gordon. Very pleased to meet you."

Ginny answered by simply saying, "Hello," but then added, "Are you sure we have to do this?"

Dr. Gordon said, "From what my nurse told me it would be wise to do an exam and do some testing. But, I can't force you to let me do this. If you think there is no chance that you could have been given an infection, you may decline it. We can then talk about your desire for birth control." The nurse added, "Did you want your mother to be in here?"

Ginny thought, *there is no way that I am going to be able to keep this a secret from my mom if she comes in. Anyway, Collin said that he had never had sex before so why should I need to be checked for infection?* So, she told the nurse that she did not think it was necessary for her mother to be in the room and then told the doctor that she was not worried about infections since it was the first time for both her and her boyfriend. The doctor then proceeded to explain the different birth control methods that Ginny had just reviewed and gave her the success rates and side effects for each, and whether they at times acted to cause abortion rather than prevent fertilization. Ginny wanted to try a hormonal method but nothing long–lasting and decided on the vaginal ring since she would not have to remember to take it each day. She was instructed by the nurse practitioner on how to place it and actually practiced putting a fake ring inside her and then taking it out. The nurse practitioner had checked to make sure it was in correctly, congratulated Ginny on placing it correctly, and then let Ginny remove it. Ginny was then instructed to wait until the first day of her next menstrual period before she placed her first contraceptive ring.

Five days came and went. Ginny waited a few more days and still no period. Her breasts were now a bit more painful than when she was at the doctor's office. She decided to wait a few more days but wondered how she could be wrong since the nurse agreed with her as to when she should expect her next flow. Still a few more days later and still nothing. She had heard that stress could cause a late, or missed period, and she knew she was stressed about it not coming, so she brushed it off on that. But, she was also wondering why she seemed to be going to the bathroom more frequently. She decided to go on–line to see if she could find out what all this meant but she didn't at all like what she found. From the symptoms she was having the first diagnosis listed was PREGNANCY. She freaked and silently pleaded, *this can't be. God, don't let me be pregnant.* She didn't know what to do next. *I need to get a pregnancy test. No, I need to talk to Jenny. No, no one can know until I know for sure. But where should I go to buy the test. I don't want to be recognized. My dad is going to hate me and I'm really going to upset my mom. She told me to come to her, and I didn't. I told Collin it would be okay.* She started to cry and rushed into the bathroom so no one could hear her. Her mind continued to race and then she finally settled down. Still wiping away her tears, Ginny convinced herself that she should not jump to conclusions. She decided she needed to have a pregnancy test, because if she were pregnant, she had to come to grips with it, sooner and not later. If it were negative, she would have the greatest weight she ever carried off her chest. She went back on–line to find out where she could have a pregnancy test done anonymously because she did not want to be recognized buying a test. She found that she could go to several different places but chose one that was at least one half hour from where she lived, hoping that no one there would recognize her or her name.

The next day after her mother arrived home from work, Ginny asked her if she could borrow her car to pick up a few things she needed for school. Her mother told her that she could, but wanted to know when she would be back since dinner would be at six. Ginny told her that she would be home in time for dinner. Then she thought that if she went to the clinic that she planned to go to it might take her more time if they started to ask questions, and she just wanted to have the pregnancy test and be done with it. So she decided to drive to the next town over and look for a drug store. She figured she could get some supplies for school in case her mother asked her what she bought, and she could also get the pregnancy test at the same time.

When she got to the drug store she took time to look at the person working the check–out counter to make sure she didn't know them and proceeded to the aisle with the pregnancy tests. She was in a daze as she read the packages to find out how to do the test. She had decided that she was going to go to a department store and use the bathroom to do the test so that she could dispose of the packaging in their trash. Ginny found a test that would only take at most five minutes to give the result and that she could afford. Now she just had to get some school supplies. She bought some highlighters and some colored paper for her printer and felt that should get her by if her mom asked what she went for. She hated that she had to be deceptive since she never had done that before. A wave of nausea hit her and she wanted to vomit, but she caught her breath and was able to stave it off. She asked herself, *what is happening to me? This isn't me! I feel horrible having to sneak around and now I feel sick!*

She stuck to her plan though, going next to a nearby department store to do the pregnancy test. She opened the package in a stall and read the directions again. She found that there were not one but two tests in the package and wondered why. She was worried that she did not have a container to put some of her urine in and was very relieved when the instructions said that she could urinate directly on the test strip. She grimaced thinking about how gross this was going to be. *I am going to end up peeing on my hands,* she thought. Ginny was now shaking with nervousness. She picked up one of the test strips and with her legs widely separated on the toilet seat she held the strip with her trembling hand, positioned it, and started to urinate. She then dropped the strip in the toilet bowl. "Oh crap!" she said, startling the woman in the next stall. She forced herself to stop her stream and quickly grabbed the second test. *Okay, get ahold of yourself,* she admonished herself. She placed the second strip with a much more steady hand and started her stream again.

It didn't take long before the test strip showed a plus sign. Ginny didn't want to believe it. She wished she hadn't wasted the other test, but when she got up from the toilet seat she looked into the bowl and she could see the other strip, now staring at her, with the same positive sign. She was shaking again and then started to sob. *What am I going to do? I'm so stupid! My dad will kill me if he finds out. I worked so hard on my grades to earn his love over this past year. There is no way that he can find out about this. I let mom down too. But I thought that I was on my period. How did this happen? I told Collin that it was safe! I can't mess up his life.* Another woman who had walked into the bathroom and heard the continued sobbing asked Ginny if she was okay, and Ginny answered whimpering, "I'll be okay." The woman answered, "Are you sure?" and Ginny said again tearfully, "Yeah." *This is all my fault!* With that last thought she secured in her mind what she needed to do. She in no way knew that Collin had been receiving the sext messages and what effect they had on him. She simply felt that the burden of what happened was all on her. With a sense of emptiness and dread she tried to wipe the tears from her eyes as best she could as she left the store and drove home wondering how she was going to keep herself together at dinner.

Chapter Eighteen

Ginny told her mother she wasn't feeling well and that she didn't feel like eating. It didn't take much in the way of acting like she was sick since she was a mess psychologically now and had lost most expression from her face which made her look sick.

"What's the matter?" Rose asked.

"My stomach isn't feeling too good," Ginny replied. That was not totally untrue since her worry had caused some upset and certainly some was caused by the early pregnancy.

"I'll get you something to feel better," Rose offered as she went to find some Pepto Bismol.

Rose returned quickly and offered to give Ginny a dose, but Ginny told her that she'd bring it upstairs with her and take it there. She really didn't know if she would, but decided to make it look like she did. She was more like a zombie than a person now as she poured some in a spoon and then dumped it down the sink leaving the stained spoon on the bathroom counter.

She then did a google search for *ways to end a pregnancy* and what she found started to make her cry and panic again. Not only did she not have the money to pay for it, but she had to be eighteen to have the abortion without needing to have a parent consent to it. She became nauseous and sweaty and then fainted, falling off her chair and onto the floor. Rose was just outside her door when this happened and heard her hit the floor. Rose shouted through the door,

"Ginny, are you okay?" There was no sound and Rose quickly pushed open the door and found Ginny on the floor. Rose screamed for Alex, causing Alex and Marty to run up the stairs and into the room. Alex shook Ginny and shouted, "Can you hear me?" Ginny opened her eyes and tried to say something but the words didn't make any sense. Alex told Marty to get a glass of water while Rose went to get a cold wash cloth to wipe Ginny's forehead. Gradually Ginny started to make some sense. She took a drink of water and then asked, "What happened?"

"We don't know for sure but it looks like you passed out. I was outside your door when I heard a loud thump in your room, and you didn't answer when I called to you," Rose said. She then added, "You scared me half to death! How do you feel now?"

"I feel better now, but I feel hungry, and mom, I need to talk to you."

When Alex heard that he thought that it must be one of those 'female things', and since Ginny seemed to be doing alright, he let them be alone.

Ginny came to realize that she wasn't going to be able to deal with her problem alone. She knew that she had made herself sick with worry because she didn't know how to handle the situation.

Rose helped Ginny change into her pajamas and into bed and told her that she would be right back with some of tonight's dinner. Ginny said, "Can you make that just toast and tea, mom?"

Rose came back with what Ginny asked for and said, "This is what I always gave you when your tummy hurt when you were real little." Ginny started to eat and Rose asked, "What did you want to talk about?"

Ginny dropped her head slightly in embarrassment and as tears started to well in her eyes she said, "Mom, I never . . ." and she started sobbing. Rose moved the tea and toast out of the way, sat on the bed with Ginny and cradled her in her arms. Ginny had meant to say that she never got her period, but when she started to talk again, she said, "Mom, I never meant to do anything wrong. I'm really sorry."

"What do you mean, honey? What did you do wrong?"

"Mom, I never got my period!" and Ginny started to cry again.

Rose was a bit flustered, and at first didn't know what Ginny was trying to say, and then it hit her. "Oh my God!" she said as she closed her eyes trying to deal with what she came to realize.

Rose asked gently, "When did this happen and do you know for sure?"

"I did a test and it was positive," Ginny said through sniffles. "That is why I asked you for the car."

Rose was angry and frustrated but the only thing she could do was hug Ginny harder. She said, "We do need to tell your father." Ginny gasped, but Rose added, "We need to discuss this together and that includes your father. You stay here and if you haven't started praying, start!" Rose had intended for Ginny to pray for guidance on how to deal with this predicament but Ginny actually was praying that her father was not going to kill her.

Rose went back downstairs. Alex said, "I guess you got all that under control."

Rose waited a few seconds and then said, "Not really."

Alex was surprised by Rose's comment and answered, "What do you mean, not really? Is she coming down with something?"

"Will you promise me you will stay calm?"

"What do you mean, Rose?" Alex asked confused but with a sense of foreboding.

"Ginny says she's pregnant."

"Pregnant! Pregnant! What do you mean pregnant! Didn't you take her to the doctor?" Alex said in rage. Ginny could hear her dad and was cringing with every syllable. She was hiding under her covers, shaking, just waiting for him to come into her room.

Alex was now pacing back and forth in the living room in disbelief. His jaw was clenched so tightly that you could see the muscles in his jaws and neck ripple. He restrained himself from confronting Ginny because although he was mad as hell he didn't know what to do or what to say. But he finally did say, "Who the hell did this to her? Was it Collin? Damn, I trusted that kid!" And as if betrayed, in a pleading tone he added, "I trusted Ginny!" He paced even more agitatedly and then, worn down mentally and crying internally, he slumped down into his chair. He then leaned forward, put his head into his hands, and just sat . . . not making another sound.

Rose now came to Alex and put a hand on his back gently but fearfully. She wasn't sure if this was going to cause him to erupt again, but he had already retreated into resignation. He sat still. "Honey, you know we need to help her," Rose said softly.

As Alex turned his head to look at Rose he noticed that Ginny was on the other side of the room and she was shaking like a leaf. Ginny said to her dad very demurely and with tears running down her cheeks, "I'm sorry daddy! Trust me, I didn't think this was going to happen."

"Why didn't you go to your mother like you said you would?" Alex tried to ask sternly but couldn't because his daughter appeared so fragile and in need. He then asked with the hope that this was all a misunderstanding, "Are you absolutely sure that you are pregnant, because if you aren't sure we had better make sure now?"

Rose said, "She told me that she did a test and it was positive."

"The test could have been wrong! Don't those tests come out wrong sometimes?" Alex said with hope.

"I suppose they do," answered Rose. "I'll call the doctor's office and see if they can do a test for her. Ginny, do you have anything after school tomorrow, because if they can fit you in we can do that after I get home?"

"No I don't, mom. I'll come right home from school."

Ginny was afraid to tell them that the test strip that she lost in the toilet bowl also showed a positive sign, but she was still hoping that this was a big nightmare and maybe she'd be told that she wasn't actually pregnant after all. So, Ginny agreed to go with her mother the next day.

Alex then asked, "If you are pregnant, who is the father?"

Ginny was actually surprised that there was even a question as to whom, but realized that since she broke her parents trust they couldn't be certain that she wasn't doing other things that they wouldn't approve of, such as sleeping around.

"Dad, I only did it once! We got carried away!" She thought about how good it had felt, but she couldn't say that to her parents. Anyway, that memory was quickly fading with all the anxiety she was now experiencing. She felt like her life was quickly being sucked away.

"So, was it Collin?" her dad asked.

And meekly Ginny answered, "Yes."

"Does he know . . . ? . . . I suppose we better wait until we find out for sure." Alex, irritation showing, then added, "I guess we can kiss off a good night's sleep tonight."

***

On her lunch break Rose was able to schedule an appointment for Ginny to at least have a pregnancy test at the doctor's office. She then texted Ginny to be ready to go to the doctor as soon as she arrived home from work.

Ginny had a little nausea when she awoke in the morning. It soon dissipated and she was very glad for that. She was also glad that the morning was busy and she had little time to think about what she was going to do after school. As the afternoon drew on she found herself daydreaming more about what was going to happen if the pregnancy test at the doctor's office was positive. She snapped back from her daydreaming when her American History teacher asked, "Ginny, are you paying attention?" She didn't hear and the student sitting behind her nudged her, making her turn around.

"What?" Ginny asked.

"Over here," her teacher said, and Ginny turned back around and stared at him.

"I said, what president was it that vetoed the renewal of the Second Bank of the United States because he felt that the common man would be adversely affected by its renewal, thereby resulting in a period of *free banking*?

Luckily she remembered and answered, "I believe it was Andrew Jackson."

Her teacher said, "You believe correctly! Now, no more daydreaming. Pay attention!"

She finished the day with no more embarrassing situations, but still found it difficult not to have her mind wander off.

***

Ginny had started to do her homework while she waited for her mother to arrive home from work, and then Collin called.

"Ginny, is there anything wrong? I haven't seen you in a week and you haven't been answering my calls!"

"Collin, I've been busy and I have a lot of homework to do."

"I know, but I thought that I was helping you. Don't you need the help anymore?"

Just then Ginny's mother arrived and said, "Ginny, I'm home. Let's go!" Ginny told Collin that she had to go somewhere with her mother and she promised she'd call him back. She just didn't tell him when, because she hadn't figured out what she was going to do if today's test was positive. She kept on praying, *please, Lord, don't make it be positive, please!*

Ginny had saved her first morning urine on the advice of her mom and had kept it in the refrigerator until she left for the doctor's office. When she and her mom got there, a nursing assistant took her urine and used a test strip to check for pregnancy. She said to Ginny and her mom, "This should only take a few minutes." It didn't even take that. It was positive within a minute. Ginny was asked to come to an exam room and was asked if she wanted her mother to come too. Ginny indicated that she did, and soon after being

173

shown to a room the nurse practitioner came in to give them the result. "It was positive," saying it almost apologetically because she thought due to Ginny's age that *positive* was not what Ginny, or her mother, wanted to hear.

Rose had been quite prepared for this result although she was wishing for a negative one. Ginny was heartbroken again and felt the anxiety well up in her like it did the day before, when she did the test herself. Tears once more came to her eyes and she said, "Mom, what am I going to do?" She was hoping that her mother would attempt to comfort her, but that did not happen.

The nurse practitioner intervened and said, "Let me see if I have anyone else waiting to see me. If not, I will give you your options. Wait right here."

In her absence Ginny became hysterical and said, "I've got to have an abortion. How can I be pregnant now? I will be too embarrassed! I'll never live this down at school!"

As Rose tried to calm Ginny down, the nurse practitioner returned and told them that they were lucky and that she didn't have another scheduled patient for half an hour. The nurse checked Ginny's medical chart and said, "I remember, didn't we give you a prescription for the birth control ring recently?"

Ginny answered in the affirmative and told her that she never got to use it because she never got her period like she thought she would. The nurse inquisitively asked more about what her last period was like, and when she was told that it was lighter than usual, she told Ginny that what she probably had was a slight bleed when she was ovulating and it must have fooled her. Ginny indeed did feel quite the fool, but also felt that it was a cruel joke. A wave of anger swept over her for having had her body deceive her.

The nurse practitioner began to explain that there were several options that could be taken. The first would be to continue the pregnancy, receiving prenatal care at their office with delivery at the hospital. She could choose to keep the baby and raise the child herself. And then the nurse asked, "Is the father of the baby involved?"

Ginny hesitated answering the question and finally Rose interjected saying, "At this time the father . . ." and she almost choked on the word, *father,* because Collin, like Ginny, was not prepared to handle parenthood, ". . . doesn't know about it."

The nurse continued saying, "I was going to say that if the father of the baby is supportive and can help you with the pregnancy and raising the baby after the birth, you can choose to raise the baby yourselves, otherwise you may want to think about adoption. The other choice would be to have an abortion. Since you are still early in the pregnancy, you would have a choice of a medical, versus a surgical, abortion."

All these things Rose knew except for the medical abortion part. She was only aware of the surgical type. Ginny knew what she wanted to do because she had already decided that before. Besides, it was legal, so it must be okay. Rose was torn. She felt in her heart that abortion was not right and her religious beliefs told her that it was not right. *But Ginny is so young and she definitely is not ready for this responsibility*, she told herself.

Ginny quickly responded when the nurse finished with the choices, "I'll have the abortion!"

Rose responded by saying, "Hold on Ginny, I'm not sure about this," but Ginny then said, "Mom, this is my life and my body! Shouldn't I get to choose?"

The nurse could see that this was not going to be resolved quickly and suggested that they take some literature home concerning both medical and surgical termination and then get back to her. She indicated that the medical abortion would have to be attempted within the next two weeks based on her true last menstrual period to have a good chance of success, so they should not delay in discussing what they were going to do.

***

It was certainly not a silent ride home. Ginny persisted in saying, "I have to have this abortion, mom! You know that I can't take care of a baby. I don't even know how! How am I supposed to do that and go to school? I don't know how to take care of a baby!"

"Honey, I can see how you feel but it just isn't right to take this baby's life. Have you thought about that? What if I did that to you?"

"Maybe that would have been better! I wouldn't have to deal with what is happening now!" Ginny protested. She was in self–preservation mode now, not thinking of her Christian upbringing, but rather in denial of it, and thereby blunted to the reality that there was a living being actively growing inside of her.

"What if your father and I helped you to take care of the baby and to raise it?" Being honest, she added, "I'm not sure how we would do that, but we could try to find a way."

"I have enough problems trying to study and do my homework, and what about my cheerleading? When am I going to have time to take care of a baby?"

"Honey, sometimes you just have to make sacrifices." Rose was not only thinking realistically in order to persuade Ginny from taking her baby's life, but she was also thinking of the sacrifices that Alex made to help his mother out when his father died, and even her own sacrifice to work two jobs to be able to provide more for her children.

Ginny didn't quite get what she was possibly supposed to sacrifice. She could not fathom that she may have to stop cheerleading and devote time to raising a child.

Ginny was quiet for some time, and then said, "Where would Collin fit into this? We haven't even mentioned him. I don't even want to tell him!"

"Don't you think he should know? Don't you think he should have a say in this, especially if you want to have an abortion? What if he doesn't want that to happen?"

Ginny was fighting not to tell her mother, but couldn't keep it back, and finally said, "Mom, I told you that it was all my fault! I told Collin that we were safe. I thought I had started my period! It's all my fault and Collin has all these plans! He's even been offered scholarships to play quarterback from three different universities. He shouldn't be punished for my stupidity!" In her own mind she was thinking that Collin wouldn't be able to proceed with the plans that he had if she were to keep the baby since they had already discussed that a *mistake* would disrupt their lives.

They arrived home but continued the conversation as they walked to the house. Rose could understand Ginny's reluctance to tell Collin but she felt that the baby was still his too, regardless of Ginny wanting to take all the responsibility. When they got inside the house, Alex was there, and Rose and Ginny's conversation stopped abruptly.

Alex asked, "What was the result?" Even before they answered he pretty much guessed the answer since there was silence. Alex said resignedly, "So, you are pregnant."

Ginny began to argue her point again with her mother, and Rose, raising her voice then said, "Okay, then how about adoption?"

"Collin will still know, mom! You know I'm going to get fat! How am I supposed to hide it from him?"

"So, you just have to tell him. I told you that he should know." Then Rose changed gears and said wishfully, "If you don't tell him you'll probably be out of school for the summer before you show much at all. You don't have to see him in the summer, and before you know it, he'll be off at his university. You'll deliver and be back to your old self before you know it, and if you do see him again, he'll never know."

Ginny looked at her mother, stunned. "Are you serious?"

Alex interjected, "It's obvious that you are arguing what you are going to do with the baby. Rose, you think adoption is the right answer? How is she to continue school and how are we going to live this down?"

"See, mom, I've got to have an abortion!"

"Now, wait a minute. I didn't say anything about abortion!" Alex clarified and then said, "Christ, how did you get yourself into this?"

Rose answered that question for Ginny by relating to Alex that Ginny and Collin got carried away and that Ginny thought she was safe because she thought she was at the start of her menses. Alex was still pissed off, but had realized he wasn't going to change what had happened and was prepared to deal with it.

"I think we had all better sit down and figure this out. But Collin has got to know!"

"Dad, I don't want him to know. It wasn't his fault!"

"Bull, how is it not partly his fault? It takes two to tango! You both promised us that it wasn't going to go this far!"

"We're not going to get anywhere if we keep this up," Rose said in frustration. "I don't know about you but I am starving. I need to eat something. It may help me think better. Maybe it will make us all think better." So they ordered out and attempted to reconcile what should be done over dinner. "Okay, we know that Ginny wants to just end the pregnancy, but I can't agree to that. You can't just kill your baby because the pregnancy isn't convenient for you. This pregnancy isn't convenient for us either. Whatever we have to do to take care of this baby we will. Won't we honey?" Rose directed the last comment to her husband.

Alex responded, "How are we going to do that? You work two jobs and I am dead tired when I get home as it is! Plus, I work every other Saturday and extra when I am needed. We can't be home all hours to take care of a baby."

And Ginny said, "I'm not going to school pregnant. I would be too embarrassed!"

"How about on−line classes? Is that a possibility?" Rose countered. "That way you won't have to go to school and risk being embarrassed.

"What is everyone going to say when I don't show up at school, especially Collin? Am I not supposed to leave the house? Besides, everyone will still find out when they see me with a baby!"

Rose then said, "It isn't that unusual to be pregnant while in high school and still go to school. Can't we just go through with it?"

"That's easy for you to say, mom. You aren't the one who has to go to school!"

Alex finally said something. "And you don't think it's going to be hard and embarrassing for your mother and me with everyone knowing that it is our daughter that let this happen? Maybe the only real solution is for Ginny to have the abortion."

Rose was aghast. She understood that Alex mostly went to church because she, herself, wanted to, but she didn't think that he would agree with Ginny on this issue. "Are you serious," she said in disbelief.

"Sure I'm serious. It doesn't appear that there is any other way to deal with this from what I have heard so far. Heck, it's not like she's so far along that it's really going to matter. I won't stop you, Ginny."

"For the love of God, you can't do that!" Rose said as tears now formed in the corners of her eyes.

Alex and Ginny now stared at Rose in dismay. "What are you so upset about? There can't be much there. You can't even tell that she's pregnant," Alex said in his and Ginny's defense.

"I don't care if you can't tell. She knows, and we know! I can't let either of you destroy something that we have no right to destroy. It is a life!"

Ginny was now sitting and just listening as her parents argued back and forth.

"You say we have no right but the law says we do, or she does, as long as I give her consent."

"This isn't a legal thing," Rose protested. "It isn't right! I don't believe my God would want us to allow her to do this. Ginny, you would be taking this child's life!"

Ginny was now thoroughly confused as to what to do, but she still didn't see keeping the pregnancy as solving anything and persisted with her father to allow her to have the abortion. In the end Rose said, "Alex, if you allow her to do this I don't know what I am going to do. Please don't. How about we sleep on it and talk about it again on Sunday when we're all free to talk about it again?"

***

Ginny called her doctor's office and found out that they would be willing to give her the medications needed to terminate the pregnancy. She would first need to come in for an ultrasound to determine exactly how many weeks along she was since the medicines were not recommended if she were too far along. But they couldn't get her in for a week and the total cost was going to be more than at an abortion clinic. Ginny decided to call the closest family planning clinic that offered abortion and found one in the next county. They told her that they take 'walk-ins'. She could come in any time before seven p.m. and they could do the ultrasound, give her the medications and then be on her way. Alex and Ginny waited for Rose to leave for work at the restaurant on Friday of that week and headed out to the clinic. They got there with half an hour to spare. Ginny only had to wait fifteen minutes to be seen after having filled out paperwork and having her father cosign the consent. Ginny was led to an exam room where she was asked to disrobe from the waist down. She had already done that once so was now used to it. It was explained to her that an ultrasound would be done by placing a skinny probe into her vaginal canal in order to see the pregnancy and determine how far along she was. She would then be given the medications if she was nine weeks along or less, otherwise she would require a surgical termination. Ginny was asked if she understood and if she had any questions. She understood and agreed to everything. The doctor placed the lubricated sterile–sheathed probe deeply into her vaginal canal and manipulated it so that the space in her uterus could be seen. Soon the doctor was able to identify a structure within Ginny's uterus and asked if she wanted to see it. Ginny wasn't certain that she wanted to and expressed that to the doctor. She was told that she didn't have to look, but she needed to be told what was seen. The doctor then described that a yolk sac could be seen and also a five millimeter tiny tissue mass with a very faint heartbeat. Ginny thought, *a heartbeat!* All she could see was the image of her mother crying, but she quickly erased that from her mind when the doctor said, "Good, you are less than nine weeks. I can give you the medicines if that is still what you want to do."

Ginny just wanted this to be over with. She was given the two medications, instructed on their use and told to return in two weeks for another ultrasound to make sure that everything was fine. She was handed some things to read and she and her father left. Rose knew nothing of what had transpired and Alex was grateful for that.

On the way home Ginny read over the medication instructions. There was also a page letting her know what to expect and a number to call if things didn't seem to be going as planned.

On arriving home she opened the bottle that contained the first tablet and without giving it another thought placed it in her mouth and washed it down with a glass of water. The instructions then said that she should use the next tablets three days later and to place them vaginally. That would be Monday. She had hoped that this could have been done before having to discuss plans again with her mother since she didn't know how she was going to hide that she had already started the process of the abortion from her. She wondered how she could have become so deceitful and she hated herself for it. The instructions also said that she could get nauseous from the pills that she would put in her vagina, and if that happened she could take the pills in the small brown envelope if needed, one every six hours, by placing them under her tongue and letting them melt. Soon afterward to several hours later she would begin to feel cramping and start to have bleeding that could be like a period or worse, and to make sure she had a good supply of maxi–pads for this. The instructions finally said that this bleeding could last for several hours, and if the bleeding was so bad as to be flowing like a faucet or if she began to get very light headed she was to call the clinic. If no one answered at the clinic she was to go to the nearest hospital emergency room. Ginny thought, *Are they kidding? What did I get myself into?* But it was too late. She had already started the process of disrupting the nutritive lining supporting her fetus inside her uterus.

Monday arrived without much incident. The weekend had gone well and Ginny had even gone to cheerleading practice without incident. She did notice a small amount of blood on her panties on Saturday after practice but she did not feel any cramping. On Sunday, she went to church like she always did with her parents and brother, but something had been different. It was different for Alex too. No one else knew that there was a difference, but Ginny and Alex could sense it. They were apathetic to the service and any prayers that they said seemed empty. After they all got home from church they made sure that Marty was busy doing something else and started to discuss the pregnancy again. Rose was elated when both Ginny and Alex said they would go along with her and not do anything drastic. Rose had said she researched on–line schooling and that Ginny could do that if she wanted rather than going to classes at the high school, but Ginny said that she wanted to stay in school and said she would just have to deal with any ridicule. Rose was flabbergasted by this sudden change of heart and thanked

God for answering her prayers. Little did she know the sequence of events that had already been initiated.

It was now time for Ginny to complete the medication protocol and wait for the effects. It took three hours and the cramping and bleeding came as advertised. Ginny had never had period cramps this bad before and her attempts at taking any pain medication was useless since she was so nauseous that she rapidly vomited the pills back up. She tried the nausea pills from the small brown envelope which helped, but did not relieve it completely. Rose heard her daughter vomiting and went into Ginny's room finding her in the fetal position trying to control the cramping. "What's wrong sweetie?" asked Rose.

Chapter Nineteen

Elsa initially sipped her opium and rum cocktail, but with the amount that she had to drink, it would have taken her an hour to consume. She therefore threw her head back and swallowed the rest in one gulp. It didn't take her long to start feeling serene and tired. Abigail Torquet helped her to lay down and arranged the pillow under her head. She also made sure that Elsa's chemise was pulled high enough so as not to soil it. She then placed the vaginal device that made it easy for her to see Elsa's cervix and then grasped her cervix with a long metal instrument on which she pulled outward toward her. With steady outward pressure she placed a small caliber rod into Elsa's womb. After a few minutes she placed a larger one, and she repeated this until the opening in her cervix was large enough to place a hollow metal tube through which she infused, with the aid of a large brass syringe, the mixture of salt and water. She allowed the mixture to stay in Elsa's womb, and then used the syringe to suck out the contents. She repeated this process, of placing the salt water and sucking it out, several times. The retrieved fluid was bloody and with pale–red fibrous strands. On the last suction of fluid there was what looked like a bubble, the size of a Liberty Dollar coin, and within the bubble, a female fetus with its head turned slightly to the side, as if looking away, and the palms of her hands and soles of her feet appearing as if they were pushing away.

Chapter Twenty

"I think I'm having a miscarriage," Ginny answered while grimacing in pain. Rose looked at Ginny's bottom and she could see blood staining her clothing.

"I think we need to get you to the hospital."

"Mom, it's alright. I think I can handle it." Ginny did not think that she was bleeding as heavily as the instructions warned about and she wasn't feeling light headed.

"Let me get you some pain medication."

"Mom, I already took some. I'll be okay."

"Then let me help you into bed and let me help you change out of those clothes."

Ginny kept the anti–nausea pills handy by her bed in case she needed them again. The cramping continued with some intensity for a couple of hours and then gradually started to improve. The bleeding also started to slow down. It was midnight before Rose felt that all was okay and she could get to sleep herself. Ginny had already fallen asleep but she would dream–a dream about the son she would have had.

***

Rose woke early the next day and checked to see if Ginny was alright before she had to leave for work. Ginny said that she was tired but otherwise did not feel too bad. "It looked like you lost a lot of blood last night. Are you sure you feel strong enough to go to school today?"

"I think so, mom," answered Ginny.

"Let me make you a good breakfast, and, oh, I have some vitamins with some iron. Maybe it would be good for you to take one for a couple of weeks to get your strength back up."

Ginny devoured the breakfast and took the vitamin and got ready for school. She didn't feel that she was ready to get back to the physical exertion it took to do her cheerleading or P. E. class so she decided to explain to her coach and P. E. teacher that she had just had a very heavy period and didn't feel up to par. She asked if she could take a few days off until she felt better. Neither one of them had a problem with her request, and it worked out great for her because she ended up going to a study hall during her P.E. class and was able to catch up on the work she didn't do the previous night due to her self-induced illness.

After school, even though she didn't work out with the other cheerleaders, she did watch from the stadium stands. Of course she had to explain to the other girls why she wasn't practicing because they all wanted to know, and of course, she had to listen to everyone else's horror stories of their sometimes heavy menstrual periods. They were doing most of their workouts and cheer practice outdoors and it just so happened that the track team had just recently started practicing. She was therefore able to see Collin work out. She waited until practice was over and tracked him down. Collin wanted to know what had happened to her since he hadn't spoken to her for at least five days. He asked her, "Why didn't you call me back like you said you would?"

Ginny answered, "I wasn't feeling well and had to go to the doctor. But it's alright now. I took some medicine and I feel much better now." As she was saying that, she saw the image of the baby boy from the dream she had the prior night and got a chill down her spine.

Collin said, "Are you sure you feel better? It looks like you just saw a ghost or something."

Ginny recomposed herself and told Collin that she just had a chill but was feeling fine.

"I didn't see you practicing today. How can you be fine?"

"I just asked for a few days off so that I can get my strength back. The coach was okay with that."

Collin offered to take Ginny home if she would wait for him to shower and change. Ginny knew her father would be home and called him to let him know that Collin would be bringing her home. Collin's name caught Alex off guard. It irritated him. He knew that Ginny had said that it was her fault that she ended up pregnant but he couldn't stop from also blaming Collin. Yes, the problem was taken care of, but Alex could not forgive Collin for betraying his trust. Alex said to Ginny, "I'll come and get you. You just wait for me. I am not going to be a fool a second time." Ginny started to get tense, feeling her father's irritation.

"But dad, we won't do it again." But, as she was saying that her father hung up and she realized she wasn't going to be able to convince her father. And she knew the whole reason she wanted birth control in the first place was that she could not trust herself to be chaste, but she did not want to believe that now. She just wanted to be with Collin but could sense it all falling apart.

When Collin finally finished dressing after his shower he came outside, only to find Ginny gone.

***

Ginny was no longer allowed to talk to Collin or see him alone. The newfound friendship that she thought she had created with her father when they agreed on the abortion was only an ether and she was now back to the harshness of reality, the reality of breaking a trust and the subsequent consequences.

Oh, she did meet Collin, but secretly now. But she also found that any time that he tried to kiss her his kisses were not as warm and satisfying as they had been before. Collin was not at fault for that. It was her. Collin had no knowledge of the pregnancy or the abortion. All he remembered was the bliss of the moment when they relinquished their virginity. Ginny could only remember the pain that transpired since then and their kisses lost any of the specialness that they had had. She had no one now to console her pain for she had no one that she felt she could speak to about this. She couldn't tell her mother, whom she could always rely on to listen and comfort her in the past, because she had deceived her into thinking she had a miscarriage rather than an abortion, and her mother had been dead set against an abortion. She couldn't get comfort from Collin because she was never going to tell him that she had aborted his child, for what if she were wrong and he would have accepted the pregnancy? Could she tell her brother Brian? She thought about that but didn't want to risk having it spill out to her mother in the future. She certainly didn't want to lay the burden of knowing what she'd done on Marty and she didn't believe he could help her anyway. She thought of Jenny. She was her best friend, and even though she did not feel it was a good idea to tell Jenny and seek her opinion when she found out she was pregnant, she had no one else and nowhere to turn now. She felt utterly alone. She asked herself, *Can I trust Jenny to keep it a secret?* All these thoughts kept spinning round and round in her head.

Alone and feeling like she was going out of her mind, she tried to sleep but found her dream was becoming more frequent and it also robbed her of the rest she desperately sought. The dream soon became a nightmare to her as she was able to see through her body as if it were transparent. She could see the interior of her womb and a pulsating heart within it. With every beat she would see first a fetus, and then gradually an increasingly developed baby, a male baby. She would then see herself smile at the baby and the child smile back at her. In the next instant her baby would turn into a pool of blood within her womb and blood would appear to flow out from it. She would awake in a cold sweat, ripping off her covers and looking for the blood.

Ginny couldn't concentrate on anything and her grades began to show it. She thought that she was losing her mind. When her father confronted her about her worsening grades she lashed out screaming, "I hate you!" She wasn't exactly sure why she had said that, but had acted instinctively and with rage. Alex was stunned. He didn't know what to say next, so he didn't say anything at all.

Ginny wouldn't look at her father, but blankly looked down at her desk. Alex remained speechless. He knew something was wrong, but didn't have the foggiest idea of what questions to ask or how to fix it. He finally asked, "Are you alright, Ginny?" But Ginny was in a daze and didn't answer.

Alex left Ginny alone and went down to talk to Rose. "Do you know what is wrong with Ginny?" In the back of his mind he knew that the recent events may have been the root cause but refused to admit it to himself.

"What do you mean, wrong?"

"She just told me she hated me and now she is just staring at her desk. Is she on drugs?"

Rose ran up the stairs to check on Ginny. "Ginny, what's wrong?"

Rose grabbed Ginny and moved her to her bed. She sat down with her, held her tightly, softly caressed her face and said, "You know you can tell me what's wrong. Everything will be alright. You can tell your mother." Still there was no response. Rose turned Ginny's face towards hers and looked in her eyes and asked, "Do you need something to eat?" Ginny finally answered, "No, I'm not hungry. I'm so tired."

"Let me get you to bed then."

"No! I don't want to go to sleep."

"What do you mean? You said you were tired."

Becoming agitated, Ginny said, "But I don't want to have that dream again!"

"What dream?" Rose asked as she tried to calm Ginny down.

"No, I don't want to see it. Don't make me go to sleep! Don't make me go to sleep!"

"I think we better get her to a hospital, Rose," Alex said. "Something's not right."

Ginny did not resist and let Rose and Alex take her down the stairs and to the car. They instructed Marty to go over to his best friend's house and stay there until they called him. They told him that his sister was sick and needed to go to the hospital. They drove to the hospital Emergency Room. When they got there they were asked what the problem was. Rose answered, "We don't know what's wrong. She just has this glazed look on her face and is scared to death to go to sleep, saying she doesn't want to have the dream again."

They were brought to a room and were told that she would be seen by the doctor soon. Before the doctor got there a young woman with a white coat came in and drew some blood from Ginny's arm. Ginny didn't make a sound and barely noticed what the girl had done. She also asked Ginny to give her a urine sample. Ginny simply looked straight through the girl's eyes. Rose finally said to Ginny, "She wants you to give a urine sample." Ginny went berserk thinking that they wanted her urine for a pregnancy test and screamed, "I am not pregnant! No, I can't be. I can't be. I want to leave! Get me out of here!" Ginny couldn't be controlled and she needed to be sedated. With her parents' permission an intravenous line was started and her wrists were restrained to prevent her from pulling the line out if she were to awake. Rose cried and wondered what was happening to her beautiful girl. Alex held onto Rose but otherwise felt helpless.

About a half hour later a doctor came in and started to examine Ginny. She was still sedated and couldn't answer questions, so the doctor just got as much information as he could from Rose and Alex. "Has she been complaining of any pain? Has she been acting unusually lately? Has anything significant happened recently that you're aware of?"

Reluctantly Rose answered, "She did have a miscarriage just recently. It happened at home." Alex stood quietly and did not utter a word.

The doctor said, "Well, I can't find anything physically wrong with her. Her vital signs are stable and I do not see any evidence of trauma. Her urine and blood tests all look normal. I need to tell you, we did do a drug screen on her and that was normal too. I'm sure you are happy to hear that. The only thing that makes sense is that she may be suffering from some type of psychological effect from the miscarriage. I would like her to be seen by our psychiatrist tomorrow."

Alex piped up, "Why not today?"

The doctor answered, "With the effects from the sedative I can't guarantee that she'll be able to answer any questions reasonably, even if she wakes up today. It would be better to wait until tomorrow. We'll put her in observation. I'm just concerned that she may be disoriented and be combative when she wakes up. Could at least one of you stay with her so she sees a familiar face when she wakes? If she isn't combative at that time, we can remove the restraints. Oh, and we can take the I V out. She won't need that."

The doctor left and Alex said, "A psychiatrist! What the hell next!" What the hell has happened? She was doing just fine until this all began!" He was referring to the pregnancy and the abortion. To Rose it was the pregnancy and the miscarriage.

They both had to be at work the next day. Alex was concerned that Rose would find out about what truly happened to the pregnancy if Ginny awakened and started to pour out to her mother. He offered to stay, but Rose said that she would stay too. There was no way that she was going to leave her darling. Alex told her that one of them should go home and get some sleep and be awake the following day in case needed at the hospital for something. Rose told him that she would sleep right there next to Ginny, even if it had to be in a chair. Alex was getting nowhere. He decided that he would stay with Rose in case Ginny woke and started to say something he thought both he and Ginny would regret. He had gone through enough already. He did not want to find out what Rose meant when she said that she didn't know what she would do if he and Ginny carried out the plan for the abortion. If Ginny was losing her mind, he didn't want to risk losing Rose too.

So, they both stayed. They called Marty to make sure he had his house key and then spoke to his friend's parents to let them know that they were at the hospital with Ginny. They didn't go into details but said that it didn't look serious and then asked if they could keep Marty for the night and make sure he got to school in the morning.

Ginny started to rouse a couple of hours later. It was now about eleven at night. She seemed calm but then reacted when she couldn't move her arms. Rose said, "You're okay, Ginny. You're in the hospital." Rose started to run her hand through Ginny's hair trying to soothe her. "You're okay. You're okay," Rose said over and over. "They had to give you some medicine to calm you down. You had become hysterical. But you look okay now," she said as she continued to run her hand through Ginny's hair.

"What happened?" Ginny asked.

"Just rest, honey." Ginny fell back to sleep since the lights were turned low to the point of being almost completely off. One of the nurses was able to secure a couple of cots and Rose and Alex were able to get some rest, at least until four o'clock in the morning when Ginny awoke suddenly and tried to throw off her sheet, but couldn't due to the restraints. She started to scream. Rose and Alex awakened and Alex fell out of the cot not remembering where he was. He got up and ran into the wall, still not recognizing where he was. Rose was already at Ginny's side calming her down. A nurse had heard the scream and ran to the room and saw that Rose had everything under control. "I think she had a nightmare." Rose whispered to Ginny asking her what caused her to scream, and Ginny answered, "I lost my baby. I lost my baby boy!" Alex was able to hear this and was relieved that Ginny did not say that she aborted her pregnancy. He was surprised to hear her say *baby boy* because he had no idea that she knew the sex and wondered how big this baby was. He began to question his consent for Ginny to have the abortion.

They remained awake until daylight. Since it appeared that Ginny wasn't any further risk to herself, or others, the doctor gave the order to have the restraints removed and indicated that the psychiatrist would be there that morning. Both Rose and Alex called work to let them know that there was a family emergency and they wouldn't be at work. That was enough said for Alex since all his fellow workers were guys, but for Rose, all her fellow workers wanted to know what the problem was. Rose simply said that she couldn't give any details, but told them she would be back the next day. She asked them to let her clients know and reschedule appointments. Rose didn't look forward to that next day back and all the questions she knew would be asked.

Ginny had already been moved to a regular hospital room before the psychiatrist got there and Rose and Ginny's nurse had already prepped her for the visit. They told her that hopefully the doctor would be able to figure out why she was having the nightmare and could figure out a way for it to go away. They knew it was a simple way to put it, but enough of an explanation to keep Ginny relaxed. Underneath what appeared externally as relaxation, Ginny was still in turmoil and confused. Her life was now upside down and she didn't know how to turn it right–side up again. She couldn't wait for someone to help her, but was anxious that the news of the abortion would destroy her relationship with her mother.

***

"Hello Virginia, I am Dr. Licht. I was asked to come talk to you and see if I could help you." Ginny had been sitting in a chair watching television with her parents and was surprised to have been addressed as Virginia. Rose was a little surprised too, since rarely, if ever, was the name Virginia used at home. Ginny looked at her mom as if to see if it was okay to speak and she could tell by Rose's eyes that she could. Ginny said, "I go by Ginny."

195

Okay, Ginny, how about we try to figure out what is bothering you so much? Is it okay if I ask your parents to let us talk alone, at least for now? Again Ginny looked at her mother, and then her father, as if to get approval for this request. Rose and Alex had already been standing when Dr. Licht entered the room and Rose prodded Alex to leave the room and said, "If you need to talk to Ginny alone, please go ahead." Dr. Licht then told Ginny's parents that there was a waiting room at the end of the hall, or they could get some fresh air, and she should be done in about an hour.

Ginny's parents left and Dr. Licht asked Ginny some mundane questions in order to relax her since she could see by her fidgeting that she was very anxious. She had already been given some baseline information from the doctor that did her intake evaluation so she could direct her questions appropriately.

"What year of school are you in now?

Still anxious, Ginny answered, "Junior."

"Are you involved in any activities or clubs outside of classes?"

Ginny was startled by her question because all she could picture was her and Collin having sex, and she sharply asked, "Like what?"

Dr. Licht, taking Ginny's guarding in stride, answered, "Like a club or sports or band."

Ginny loosened just a bit and said, "I'm a cheerleader," and added with pride, "A varsity cheerleader!" She then added, "I should be at practice!"

The doctor said, "That's okay, Ginny, they know that you can't be there today. You'll be back soon enough. How has practice been going?"

Ginny searched for the right answer. She was confused as to when she was last at practice and again said with agitation, "I'm not sure. I mean, I can't remember when I was last there."

Tears were forming in Ginny's eyes and the doctor said, "That's okay Ginny. You don't have to worry about that now."

The questions continued and Dr. Licht was able to show Ginny that she was not to be feared. Ginny ended up emotionally divulging the sequence of her nightmare, but did not let Dr. Licht know anything about the recent abortion.

Dr. Licht then said to Ginny, "Do you think your dream is related to your recent miscarriage?"

The doctor could see that Ginny was surprised when she brought up the miscarriage and attempted to keep her calm by saying, "The doctor that saw you last night informed me of this. It was important information that he needed to know when you came in last night."

Ginny broke down and cried. When asked why she was crying she said, "I'm afraid to fall asleep! I keep on having that nightmare! It never goes away! Last night was the most sleep I've had in two weeks!"

"That sounds horrible," Dr. Licht said in real sympathy, acknowledging Ginny's pain. Dr. Licht then asked, "Did you plan on the pregnancy?"

Again surprised, Ginny took time in answering and eventually said, "No, not really."

And then, Dr. Licht took a chance. She took a chance because she knew that she might strike a nerve and cause Ginny to panic. "So were you sad or happy that you lost your pregnancy?"

At first Dr. Licht thought her question had backfired as Ginny started to decompensate. Ginny's nightmare surfaced, tormenting her even though she was awake. It was so real to her that she felt like she was hemorrhaging. She looked at her crotch and imagined that she saw blood soaking through her jeans. Dr. Licht looked on in horror and surprise as Ginny feverishly attempted to remove her jeans right in front of her to look for the blood while she screamed "I killed my baby! I killed my baby boy!"

Ginny would not stop screaming and needed to be sedated again.

Dr. Licht went to look for Ginny's parents and found them in the waiting room. They asked the doctor what she thought and she informed them that she felt that Ginny had what was called Nightmare Disorder and it was related to the trauma induced by the loss of her pregnancy. She was careful not to say anything about what Ginny had last said, of killing her baby, since she was not sure what Ginny had meant by that. She was not sure whether Ginny blamed herself for the miscarriage or if she had wished for the miscarriage or whether she had actually done something to induce the pregnancy to fail. But, deep down, she knew that with a reaction like this, the loss, most likely, did not just happen.

Alex thought to himself, *What has happened to my daughter? Did I cause this to happen? I didn't intend for this. All I wanted for her was a good life, a good education. All I wanted for her was to have it easier than Rose and I. How has it all fallen apart and can it be fixed?* Alex then asked Dr. Licht, "But this can be fixed, right?"

Dr. Licht hesitated and then said, "There is a very good chance that I can get her to improve. It will take time."

"How much time are you talking about?" asked Alex.

Dr. Licht measured her next statement and followed it with a question trying to uncover any bit of information that might be hidden to her by saying, "It is hard to tell. It may help to know more specifics as to what happened with the pregnancy loss. If you know anything further, it may help her recovery and how quickly she recovers." She didn't at this time want to let them know that this could be a long process that could involve drug therapy as well as psychotherapy, but knew that she may have a tougher time with treatment if there were guilt issues over an intentional abortion.

Rose didn't know how to respond and just nodded her head and said, "Please, just help her." Alex was thinking, *I need to find a way to tell this doctor what actually happened if that is going to help Ginny but I can't let Rose know.*

Dr. Licht let Rose and Alex know that she felt it best that Ginny be admitted to the hospital for further evaluation and potentially to initiate treatment. Rose and Alex didn't feel that they could argue with that since they knew they couldn't deal with the situation. As Dr. Licht was walking away down the hall, Alex caught up with her. Rose went back to be with her daughter. He said to her, "You wanted to know if there was any more information. Is there anywhere that I can talk to you privately?"

There was a chapel off the main hallway and no one was there. "We can talk in here," the doctor said.

Alex started off by confessing, "I was trying to do the right thing! My wife doesn't know it but Ginny took medicine to cause it."

"Do you mean to cause the abortion or to cause her psychological problems, Mr. Chandler?"

Alex was caught off guard because he was consumed with rehearsing what he was going to say. Dr. Licht repeated her question and finally Alex said, "I mean she went to a clinic and they gave her medicine to use for the . . ." He didn't want to say the word abortion ever since he heard Ginny say that she could see, identify the sex. He had thought that she actually had seen the child when she aborted rather than just in her nightmare.

Dr. Licht stated, "I see that you are having difficulty finishing your thought. Can I help you or can you finish it for me?"

"Okay, she took medicine to cause the abortion," Alex answered.

"It sounds to me that you are having some personal issues yourself dealing with this. I can only suspect that you were aware of this all along since your daughter would have needed a parent's consent for this based on state law. So, when you said she went to a clinic, do you actually mean that you both went to a clinic, or are you saying that she lied about her age or they gave the medicines to her illegally?

Alex felt as though the doctor was starting to be accusatorial and answered begrudgingly and with an attitude, "Yes, I knew about it! I went with her and I signed the consent because that is what I thought she needed."

"If you consented for her why did you initially find it hard to say the word abortion? Are you now sorry that you allowed her to have it?"

Rather than directly answering that question Alex said, "I had no idea that she was going to be able to see a baby come out of her. I don't remember them telling her that! Why wouldn't they tell us that?"

"How far along was she?" Dr. Licht asked.

"I don't think she was too far along. I mean, I couldn't tell that she was pregnant."

Dr. Licht knew that Alex was not going to be useful in finding out how far along Ginny was in her pregnancy when she had it terminated, but she was interested because she felt the number of weeks along Ginny was could help her tell if the baby was far enough along to be able to tell features and genitalia. "That was important information for me to know and I thank you for it. Are you sure you are okay at this point because I'm not so sure you are?"

"I'll be alright," Alex said.

Dr. Licht tucked away the information that Alex had told her into her memory for future reference and promised herself to check on Alex's emotional stability the next chance that she had.

***

Ginny spent nearly a week in the hospital before being allowed to go back home. During that time she had further evaluations which indicated she was suffering from emotional trauma just as with post–traumatic stress. She was started on a combination of therapies which included medication to reduce the frequency of the nightmare as well as a self – rehearsed technique designed to replace her recurrent nightmare with images that were more pleasing so as to avoid the horror of her nightmare and hopefully allow her to sleep. In order to accomplish changing the nightmare to a pleasant dream she had needed to start practicing the new dream, which Ginny designed for herself, for twenty minutes each day. That was no easy feat since every time she thought about the nightmare sequence in order to replace it with something else she would often decompensate. Once she finally accomplished the task of creating the new dream, like a story board to her, she found it best to practice the new sequence of events in the evening before she became too tired. She did this because when it came to studying she would always remember what she studied better if she did it in the evening. But this was only the tip of the proverbial iceberg regarding Ginny's return to normalcy. It took weeks upon weeks of probing Ginny's psyche to isolate that it was not only the nightmares that kept Ginny from being able to concentrate and get back to her daily routine. By that time the school year had finished and she had not been able to complete her junior year of high school as she should have. She was given the opportunity to attempt to complete the work during the summer, if she was able, otherwise she was in jeopardy of not being able to graduate with her class the following year.

During her psychotherapy sessions it was discovered that although she had pretty much transitioned over to a benign dream sequence she was not able to totally extinguish the nightmare. It was as though the nightmare had burned a scar in her brain. No matter how hard she had tried to replace the images of it, she was always drawn back to it. Increasing levels of medication were tried to reduce the nightmare frequency but she began to experience numerous side effects from the medication. It became perfectly apparent that there was another force or forces that were preventing her from progressing. Ginny finally recognized, with the help of her psychologist, that she had unresolved guilt over the abortion. She had repressed her mother's horror when she had brought up abortion as a solution to the pregnancy. She had seen abortion as the only way out and knew that it was not unusual for a woman to have one. But she had not counted on how her relationship with her mother would change. Their bond just wasn't the same anymore. She had thought that it was her nightmare and her therapy for the nightmare that had changed their relationship and was hoping that over time it would improve as she, herself, got better. There was no longer any depth or quality to their relationship, and it wasn't improving as time went on. Her mother was concerned about her and continued to include her, as she always had, in meal preparation and the normal 'girl–talk'. Ginny wondered if she, herself, was the root of the problem. Ginny had already become aware that the nightmare was a consequence of the guilt she had over the abortion, but she came to realize that unless she revealed the truth to her mother, their relationship would never be the same as it had been. Ginny couldn't be certain if their relationship would ever be the same even if she did confide in her mother, but after agreeing with her psychologist as well as her psychiatrist, it was felt that if this was a key piece to resolving her problem, it was better to risk telling her mother the whole and truthful story. Ginny hadn't given thought about whether this revelation to her mother might cause a problem for her father because she had completely forgotten, or perhaps did not even internalize, her mother's response when her dad indicated that he would give consent for the abortion.

***

Alex had been concerned about his daughter's recovery and was willing to do whatever he needed to do in order to make this happen. So, when he and Rose were asked to attend a family counseling session in order to try and help Ginny's recovery, they were both more than happy to attend. Since Ginny's psyche had been so fragile, the doctors felt it best for her to have their support during what they thought would be a very trying time for her. They were not aware that it also might be a very trying time for Ginny's father.

They all met on a late Thursday afternoon at the office of the psychologist. They all knew each other, so there was no need for introductions. Dr. Licht had a chance to ask Alex

Chandler if he was doing alright since they last spoke, when she had expressed her concern for his psychological well−being. He indicated to her that his only problem was his concern for his daughter and her slow recovery. He didn't say it, but he felt that he could not now erase the events which had occurred and they all needed to get on with their lives. He had personally gotten over his concern that the pregnancy was possibly further along than he initially understood it to be. They all took seats and Dr. Licht expressed her delight at being able to all get together. She prefaced that the attempts to obtain further resolution of Ginny's condition had stalled, and from discussion with Ginny this session might be conducive to helping Ginny make some headway.

Dr. Boatright, the psychologist, first asked if anyone had anything to say or if they had any questions. Ginny had become anxious as she sat there remembering her and her father's secretive trip to the clinic for the abortive medications, and she said, "I am not sure that I can do this!"

Dr. Boatright asked, "What is wrong, Ginny? It was my feeling from you that this would be best to get this out in the open?"

"I know, I know, but . . ."

Dr. Licht could see the anxiety build in Ginny and that she was afraid of something.

"Ginny, can I talk to you a second, alone?" Dr. Licht asked. They got up and went into a smaller room and closed the door. "Ginny, you're afraid, aren't you? And it isn't your mother that you are afraid of, is it?"

Ginny confided that she didn't know exactly why she was afraid, but she had been thinking of the way that she and her father had waited to go to the clinic after her mother went to work.

"So you are afraid that if you tell your mother about having the abortion without your father knowing you are about to do this, he is going to be upset. Is that right?"

"I'm not sure exactly, but now I don't think it's a good idea for my dad to be here."

"But, you still want to tell your mom? You do see that you can't have it both ways, don't you? Your mother is most assuredly going to call your father out on this, unless she's a saint."

"Please, I need to tell my mom by myself. Let me do it alone." The pleading in Ginny's eyes convinced Dr. Licht that Ginny was probably right. They went back into the other room where Dr. Licht expressed to the others that Ginny first wanted to speak to her mother alone. Alex fidgeted for a moment as he had that feeling of helplessness once again, and then Dr. Licht said, "Mr. Chandler, how about if you, Dr. Boatright and I go down to the office entrance? There is a coffee shop down there. I think I need a cup, and I'll buy a round for the three of us." With that they left, leaving Rose and Ginny alone together. Even though Ginny should have felt tense knowing what was about to transpire, she actually felt an indescribable warmth as she finally came to the realization that her mother would never abandon her, and she said, "Mom, I need your help. I still can't get rid of the nightmare completely! I thought it was going to be okay. I thought that I could handle this alone, but I was wrong. I shut you out, but I realize that I need you more now than I ever did."

"What do you mean, shut me out, honey?" Rose said confused as she thought that Ginny never had a problem discussing things with her.

"I still can't get rid of the nightmare completely, mom, and I think I know why." Ginny's eyes started to tear. Rose reached out and brought Ginny close to her and Ginny rested her head against her mother's chest. The tears became sobs as Ginny said, "I know you didn't approve, but I had an abortion. It wasn't a miscarriage. I'm so sorry for hiding it and deceiving you." Rose too, started to cry. Her cries were first for her daughter and her pain. But they were also for the life of the child that was lost and finally for Ginny's realization of Rose's unending love for her.

Rose said to her daughter, "I love you, honey, and I will always love you. I know that you were scared to death and didn't see another way out of your problem. It's something that you should never do again."

"I know, mom. I know, now."

A weight seemed to lift off of Ginny's shoulders, but she still had concern for her dad. She asked her mom, "Are you upset with dad for helping me?"

"Yes, I am upset about that, honey. But, I know in his heart that he has always wanted the best for you. I just don't think that this was the best for anybody. And now, we have some work to do to fix things up. Would you agree?"

Ginny knew that she had to make up for the time lost at school and she knew that there would be questions about where she had been for the last couple of months. This is what she thought her mother had meant about there being some' fixing–up to do'. She answered her mother with, "I guess so mom. I think I know what you mean, but maybe I don't." She went on to tell her mom what she thought needed to be fixed and her mother explained what other things she felt needed to be fixed. They spent some time talking and agreeing about these things and decided that it may be best to bring them up today while they had both Ginny's psychologist and psychiatrist present.

***

Alex had felt very awkward going to have coffee with two professionals, but Dr. Boatright made him feel right at home by asking about his occupation. Alex opened up about how he got into the work and his disappointment of not being able to continue his education as he had hoped. In the end they started talking about cars since Dr. Boatright was an enthusiast. Dr. Boatright mentioned that as he got older and had a family his choices of automobiles became more practical. "Yeah, I drive a minivan now. Not much power and not much style, but hey, you gotta do what you gotta do. It gets the kids where they need to go, and as you probably know, that can be anywhere with sports and everything. The car I really loved, and of course I was single then, was my '85 Mustang SVO. I really loved that car." Alex got a smirk on his face and said, "An '85 Mustang SVO, are you serious?" Dr. Boatright was surprised at Alex's reaction. Alex went on to say, "Now, the '85 IROC–Z Camaro, that was a car!" They started to argue over which car was the better. Dr. Licht wished she could have hidden under the table. During the heat of the argument they were asked to leave the coffee shop because they were disturbing the rest of the patrons. They decided they would return to Dr. Boatright's office, but on the way there they continued their argument. Dr. Licht urged them both to settle it down before they entered the office. Rose and Ginny had already been talking about how Ginny would return to her old self–ironically maybe even better. Dr. Boatright knocked on his office door to check if it was okay to come back in. A jubilant voice said, "Of course you can come in." And as the trio entered, Ginny smiled her sweet smile. Alex could tell something magical had happened and smiled back at her.

None of them sat down as they began to discuss what had transpired between Ginny and Rose. Alex had figured out that the cat was out of the bag and he looked at Rose and Rose looked back at him. He could see in her eyes that she did not approve of what he had done. He would come to know that although Rose understood his intentions for what he had done, she would never accept this kind of deception ever again, and that nurturing life would be the only possibility–not its destruction.

"Ginny, you look so much more vibrant than usual. What happened between you two?" asked Dr. Boatright.

"I said what I knew I had to say all along, but I didn't have the courage to say what I needed to say until there was no way out. Nothing was working. I couldn't get better and I was losing my mom. She did nothing wrong. It was all me. I couldn't accept myself for what I had done and the nightmare kept on reminding me of that, no matter how hard I tried with the medicine and the imaging. I had no one to lean on and it was literally killing me. I was all alone and I thought that I had no one I could tell. In my own mind I was drifting further away from my support, and my main support had always been my mom. I could feel that relationship, that bond, slipping away. Not that she didn't have the love to give to me, but I couldn't give it back because I was hiding the truth from her. So, I had to tell her the truth, and she returned it with more love. That's my mom!"

Both Dr. Boatright and Licht had listened with awe. Ginny's father felt slighted, jealous and even sad, because there was no mention of any bond, no mention of any love between him and his daughter. But, Ginny added, "And dad, I know that I made a mistake. No, many mistakes. And I forced you into my first nightmare and you tried to remove that nightmare. Unfortunately it ended up with a disastrous result. I truly don't blame you for that because you reacted to my insistence. Thank you for supporting me in my time of need. I knew that mom might be upset with us both when I decided to tell her everything and I also knew that you didn't want her to know, but I just couldn't hide it from her without losing her. I know that you only tried to protect me and wished only good things for me. I do love you dad, but I have to tell you that I can't come to you as I do mom because she accepts me as I am. You seem to be convinced that the only way I'm going to be successful and happy is to ace high school and go to college. Somehow that's supposed to make everything perfect. Dad, I'm not as smart as either Brian or Marty and I need your support. Mom and I talked and I have decided to go to Cooking School after I finish high school or take the GED or whatever I need to do to graduate. It's not that I'm not going to try to do well, but I'm not going to stress out about it and I'm just going to do the best I can. I know that I do better by doing than by reading books and I've always liked and enjoyed cooking."

Ginny was looking directly at Alex as she was speaking and Alex hung onto every word that Ginny said, making eye–contact with her all the while. There was a long silence as Alex thought about what had been said. He then looked at Rose and then at Drs. Licht and Boatright before saying, "I understand what you're saying and I'll support you in what you want to try. I've been pig-headed. I realize now that I've been resentful for not going further in my own education. I just wanted you to achieve what I didn't. I was blind to the obvious stress that I now realize that I put you under. I thought I had it right in my heart, but it wasn't my heart, but rather my stubborn mind that thought it had it right." It was not easy for Alex to say, but he also said, "Please forgive my stubbornness and my pride."

Dr. Boatright thought, *This was a piece of cake. I wish all my cases would resolve this easily. But I still think the Mustang is better than the Camaro.*

Dr. Licht was smiling as she said, "It sounds like there is a plan, and some issues that we didn't even plan on pursuing today got cleared up. I would still like to see you again, Ginny. I truly wish that what happened here today helps to resolve your nightmares and your inability to concentrate, but I think you know only time will tell. I think it best that you remain on your medication. If it seems that the nightmares are lessening we can try to start to wean it. I will see you in a week, same time, same office."

Ginny hugged her mom while Alex, who was across from her, looked on. Ginny then turned and looked at her father and ran to him. She threw her arms around him and they hugged. They hugged for a very long time as if attempting to wring out all the stress that existed between them. Alex then turned to Rose and looked at her again as if seeking her forgiveness. She stepped close to him, kissed him and whispered to him. She had forgiven him. She forgave him because Rose's love for Alex would never change, nor Alex's for Rose.

Epilogue

Ginny went on with the encouragement of her parents, and Alex became a cheerleader for her as opposed to a thorn in her side. She was able to finish high school on time and graduate with her class after being allowed to finish all the missing required work for her junior year during the summer. She had continued to stay in close touch with Dr. Licht and gradually was able to wean from her medication as the nightmares gradually diminished. She continued to use the Image Therapy but even noticed that the refabricated dream that she had created was not occurring as frequently, and on the occasion that she still got the nightmare, it was less bothersome. It seemed to Ginny that getting rid of the nightmare was easier than finishing the rest of her junior year work, but she took it one day at a time and tried not to stress out. She found that she didn't need to stress out as there was no pressure to do more than she was capable of doing. Rose was always encouraging and her father learned to offer his help when she asked for it, attempting to be more concerned with helping her complete her tasks than concerned about the letter grades assigned to them. Finishing was no small feat for Ginny, but without the pressure to perform above average work, she was able to relax and get the required work done. She was then able to take the classes she needed in her senior year in order to graduate from high school. She was also able to start taking classes in the Culinary Arts which she thoroughly enjoyed, and even if she didn't always take the written tests well, she aced the practical, hands–on ones.

Collin had attempted to reach Ginny many times while she was dealing with her psychological problems, but never received any return calls or emails. It's no wonder, since

Ginny was not in any frame of mind to answer anyway. Plus, in the time dealing with her therapy she didn't have access to her cell phone or computer. Over time, Collin stopped trying to reach her and moved on. He had still been receiving the sexts from Ashley and finally succumbed and called her. They finished their senior year going out with each other, attending senior prom together, and yes, making out on numerous occasions. Collin certainly had changed as he progressed through high school, much of it due to influences along the way. He proceeded to go on to Oklahoma University on a football scholarship and was the starting quarterback for three of his four years. He then made it into the pros, playing for the Carolina Panthers for four years before suffering a rotator cuff injury to his throwing arm. His arm strength after surgery and rehab was never the same and he eventually went on to become the offensive coordinator for Texas A&M University.

And if Texas A&M reminded you of Ashley, she married Collin and became Ms. Ashley Gold–Smith soon after Collin signed his contract to play football for the Panthers. During her time at Texas A&M she started modeling, after she and a group of her fellow cheerleaders, on a dare, registered with a modeling agency. She continues to work in the Commercial Fashion Industry while continuing to finish her studies in Veterinary Medicine at Texas A&M.

Nick also went on to college and then to playing in the pros. He continues to play left offensive tackle for the Arizona Cardinals in the National Football League. Ginny's brother, Brian, finished his bachelor's degree in Engineering at Stanford and went on to complete his doctorate degree in Biomechanical Engineering and works for a Biotech firm in California. Marty, Ginny's little brother, who was always playing the latest video games, ended up with a degree and a creative career in Video-Game Animation. He also continues to play soccer in local leagues in Texas.

Rose and Alex, besides supporting Ginny with her culinary passion, continue to love each other despite the ordeal they went through with Ginny. Alex became more content and passionate with his work. He started to refurbish and rebuild classic cars at home after all the kids had been able to provide for themselves, making money less of an issue.

But, the story wouldn't be complete without knowing more of Ginny's outcome. She finished her training with high honors in all the creative and cooking aspects of the curriculum but she was average in the business aspects as you may have guessed from her earlier educational experiences. During her studies she had attracted the interest of an energetic young man by the name of Ramy Heiskanen who had been in her classes and was amazed at her food creations and her culinary presentations. He was not her equal when it came to those strengths, but he exceled in the business side of the culinary curriculum. He was a little bit older than Ginny and had had some experience in the food industry, first busing tables while he was in high school and then waiting tables and eventually learning how to tend bar before he decided to attend culinary school. He would joke around with Ginny before and after classes and they both would go out with several of the other students on the weekends to relax and have fun. He eventually asked Ginny out, and while Ginny was intent on finishing her studies and didn't want to get into any kind of relationship, she said yes, because she found him interesting, funny, and felt she could learn more about the practical aspects of the restaurant industry from him. It was a connection made in heaven. Many of their dates were to restaurants where they would critique the food presentation as well as the restaurant's ambiance and cleanliness. They would also gauge the wait staff's timeliness, politeness and efficiency. Their ratings would rarely agree on everything, especially the food, but that was mostly due to each of their individual palates. Other than the food, they would weigh the pluses and minuses and then attempt to determine what worked well together. Often they would go out with other students to restaurants recommended by their instructors and they would debate their dining experience throughout the entire evening and, at times, into the wee hours of the night.

Ginny and Ramy would often joke about opening a restaurant together seeing that their strengths complemented each other. Ramy would often say to her that she would do all the creative things, the menu and the food preparation. When Ginny would ask what he was going to do if she did all that, he would answer–"Someone has got to do crowd control since they'll be knocking down the doors trying to get in, and I'll need to count all the money!" They eventually became serious about doing it. The only problem was getting the collateral to do it. But, with the help of a small business loan, Ramy's large extended family, and Ginny's brothers, who were willing to pitch in some cash since they were both single and had some money put away, they were able to launch a successful restaurant. They put everything they learned into the venture and they thoroughly enjoyed their work as well as each other. And then one day Ramy asked Ginny to marry him. She was more than prepared. She could see their hard work paying off, and even though they had not paid off their loan for the restaurant or paid back their families, she felt secure that it was the right time and accepted his proposal.

They had a small wedding but knew they had to invite everyone in their families who helped to get their business started, and quite a few more that were unrelated, so as not to offend anyone. To Ginny and Ramy's surprise Alex had arranged to drive them away from the church in a fully refurbished 1937 Lincoln Zephyr Coupe–Sedan that he was able to borrow from a guy he had gotten to know when he started to do restorations as a hobby. Alex had always wanted to restore a car like this himself, but could never afford to. At least he was lucky to know someone who could, and did. Not only were Ginny and Ramy in their glory, but Alex was too! He was proud of his daughter, her new husband and their success, and he truly got a buzz out of driving the car. Everyone enjoyed themselves immensely at the reception and the marriage was consummated on the wedding night. There was no concern this time for whether it was the right time of month because they were more than happy to have a child in their lives and did not plan to prevent it from happening. Ginny did not conceive from that act. But, about fifteen months later she did, and on that same night she experienced yet another dream. This one revealed a tiny fetus, female, enclosed in a tiny fluid–filled bubble about the size of a Liberty Silver Dollar. At first no heart beat was visible, but in the blink of an eye the heart started to beat slowly and then faster, and then Ginny saw a smile on the baby girl's face and she saw herself smiling back. There was no fitful sleep for Ginny that night, only the pleasant dream.

There was no need for any ultrasounds during the pregnancy since the pregnancy went along smoothly. Ginny's obstetrician was surprised when Ginny told him she didn't want an ultrasound and didn't want to see if the baby was a boy or a girl. She and Ramy told him that they were going to keep the baby no matter what and wanted to be surprised when the baby was born. Ginny told her obstetrician that she felt like the baby was going to be a girl anyway, ever since her dream. She was very surprised, but not disappointed, when she delivered a baby boy. She and Ramy had picked out a boy's name just in case. They named him Aaron Michael. He was a beautiful baby and his smile was definitely Ginny's. Of course, everyone argued about the baby's other features, that is, who he resembled more, but there was no debating the smile.

Aaron received numerous gifts including the mandatory baseball glove and football even though there was no way he was going to be able to use them as a baby. He received cars and trucks as well as the usual blue onesies. Of course, he also received plenty of stuffed animals and his favorite seemed to be a very soft and squishy pure white polar bear that he always preferred to snuggle up with. He would often be found lying with his cheek against its silken ears and grasping its soft furry body with his tiny fingers.

Being in the restaurant business and having a baby was no easy feat. Ginny and Ramy were able to handle it all by bringing the baby to the restaurant in the morning hours. During food preparation, ordering, receiving, placing stock and doing the accounting he sat and played or slept in his Port-a-Crib. During business hours the grandmas were more than willing to pitch in and baby sit. Ramy's mom, Annika, usually handled the child during the lunch hours, and Rose during the dinner hours since she had quit her job at Luciana's Restaurant ever since her children had become secure enough to handle their own finances. On Saturdays that Alex wasn't working he would often volunteer to take care of Aaron for the lunch shift, leaving the dinner shift for either Rose or Annika and her husband, Arto, to fight over. They enjoyed every minute of it, and often spent time together watching him.

After the restaurant had established itself with an excellent reputation, Ginny and Ramy made the decision to reserve Sundays for themselves and their baby. They were also able to attend church services which was something they felt important to do, and wanted to do, for themselves as well as their child. There were times when one of them might have to go to the restaurant for a short time on Sunday mornings as the need arose, but most of that day was spent together as a family.

***

Three years later they had another child, this time a girl, and they named her Sophie Alana.

Sophie was very playful and expressive. Ginny and Ramy could always tell from her cries what she needed and as she developed and started school she was very talkative and made friends easily.

Aaron was very smart and inquisitive, but also more pensive and deliberate in his actions. His pensiveness always made it look as though he wasn't sure of himself. This didn't fare him well with his male peers who valued spontaneity and rambunctiousness. In many of their games he found himself as the 'odd man out', the last one picked, if picked at all. He wasn't sure what made him so much different, but he knew that he found his joy when reading history of the late nineteenth and early twentieth centuries. He would often do just that. When he was alone he would grab Frosty, his snow – white polar bear, and while reading would unconsciously slide his fingers against its silk ears.

Aaron sensed he was different in another way, also. It was a difference he could not reconcile until well into his late teenage years. He never seemed to feel right in his body. Not that he was sick, but he never felt comfortable in it. Ever since he had watched Sophie's diaper changings he had harbored a resentment for his own genitalia, but he never knew what to do with that feeling. When Grandma Annika babysat him at her house, he found that he was fond of playing with an old porcelain doll of hers. The fact was, he still enjoyed that doll. When he went with his parents for the first time to the history museum, he found himself mesmerized by the display of the late eighteen hundreds. He was especially intrigued by the garments worn by the women of that era. He also found that he could easily engage almost any female in discussion and they would be happy to reciprocate, but not so with the guys. Even with males he felt were his friends, he found conversation difficult and definitely less interesting. Ginny and Ramy had recognized that their son was not interested in the usual rough and tumble play as a small child but saw his interest in reading and encouraged it. They knew that he was intelligent. They watched as his knowledge and keen interest in history grew and were amazed at his retention relating to the past two centuries. Why that interest they did not know, but they did not see it as a problem. They saw it as a gift.

It was not until Aaron finished high school that he finally came to grips with what was truly bothering him and what he truly desired. After years of repressing his utmost desire he finally relinquished and confided to Ginny and Ramy that he felt he needed to see a doctor. They were surprised for they didn't know why. They were even more surprised when he told them he thought he needed to see a psychologist. It was exceedingly difficult for him to tell them why, but without much deliberation he just blurted it out. He told them that he needed to be a girl.

Over the next eighteen months there were a series of meetings with his psychologist. During this time he needed to prove that his desire to be female was real and was required to live as though he were a girl, or should it be said woman, for he was now eighteen. He needed to put off college during this time, which was probably best, since this enabled him to transition hormonally to his desired sex and not have to worry about that during the start of his college education. He went on to fully transition by means of surgery and then went on to finish studies in History with an emphasis on American History.

It truly was never discovered completely why she so deeply wanted to be a girl, but on reading the statistics she found that one in thirty thousand boys and one in one–hundred thousand girls desire to have sex–reassignment surgery. She also read that the usual explanations for being born into the wrong sex were that it was somehow genetic or perhaps a hormonal effect during development. Were genetics or hormone responsible for her condition or was it due to influences during her upbringing? There was also medical literature that indicated this last reason as an explanation for Gender Identity Disorder. During her discussions with her psychologist they had covered extensively her early childhood, her repulsion to her male genitalia and her ease at relating to the female gender rather than to the male. They went over her reluctance for the rough and tumble and whether that reluctance was something engendered in her by her father. Did he not inculcate any of the usual stereotypical male passions upon her? None of them, for her, seemed adequate as an explanation. She was inquisitive and asked him if he was sure there was no other possible explanation. Her psychologist told her that another explanation was always possible, but he didn't know what it would be. He did say that he had his musings about it, especially since he had certainly been intrigued about the combination of her desire for womanhood and her interest, or better said, fixation on the nineteenth century. And after being asked to share his musing, he offered, "Just suppose that there have been spirits that were meant for another time in history and somehow they just don't get born? What happens to those spirits? Where do they go?"

In the end, and with much joy, Aaron Michael officially changed her name to Eryn Michelle. Her psychologist was left to further contemplate whether there was some type of connection between Eryn's nineteenth century fixation and her gender dysphoria, for Eryn exhibited not only a passion to a bygone period in history, but an ease when talking of it and about it, as if she were meant to be in another place and time.

www.ingramcontent.com/pod-product-compliance
Lightning Source LLC
Chambersburg PA
CBHW061322200626
46813CB00017B/2790